Billion-Dollar Matches

The one thing money can't buy? Love!

Finding true love is *never* easy. But when you're famous, it's even harder... So, M is here to help! M is a dating agency with a twist. They offer, to the rich and famous, a chance to date away from the limelight. And it's this promise of absolute discretion that compels *every* A-lister to keep them on speed dial.

M's founder, Madison Morgan, is no stranger to the red carpet herself. A former child actress, Madison knows—better than anyone!—the value of privacy. Which makes her an expert at finding the *most* idyllic and secluded locations for her clients. From Lake Geneva to the Seychelles, and Puerto Rico to Indonesia, Madison creates the perfect backdrop to a couple's love story. And, just maybe, her own?

Fall in love with...

The Princess and the Rebel Billionaire
by Sophie Pembroke

Available now!

Surprise Reunion with His Cinderella
by Rachael Stewart

Caribbean Nights with the Tycoon
by Andrea Bolter

Indonesian Date with the Single Dad
by Jessica Gilmore

Coming soon!

Dear Reader,

Imagine if there was a company that could not only find you your perfect match but also arrange for you to be alone together for a full week to get to know each other—and hopefully fall in love. Sounds simple, right?

But true love is never truly simple—as Princess Isabella of Augusta and her rebel billionaire, racing car world champion Matteo Rossi, learn in this story. They come from different worlds, want different things...and neither of them even chose to be there! How can they be a perfect match?

But the M dating agency knows what it's doing. So sit back, turn the page and get whisked away to Lake Geneva, Augusta and Rome with Isabella and Matteo as they figure out what true love means and why it's worth fighting for...

Happy reading!

Love,

Sophie x

The Princess and the Rebel Billionaire

———

Sophie Pembroke

Recycling programs
for this product may
not exist in your area.

ISBN-13: 978-1-335-56702-4

The Princess and the Rebel Billionaire

Copyright © 2021 by Harlequin Books S.A.

For questions and comments about the quality of this book,
please contact us at CustomerService@Harlequin.com.

Harlequin Enterprises ULC
22 Adelaide St. West, 40th Floor
Toronto, Ontario M5H 4E3, Canada
www.Harlequin.com

Printed in U.S.A.

Sophie Pembroke has been dreaming, reading and writing romance ever since she read her first Harlequin as part of her English literature degree at Lancaster University, so getting to write romantic fiction for a living really is a dream come true! Born in Abu Dhabi, Sophie grew up in Wales and now lives in a little Hertfordshire market town with her scientist husband, her incredibly imaginative and creative daughter, and her adventurous, adorable little boy. In Sophie's world, happy *is* forever after, everything stops for tea and there's always time for one more page...

Books by Sophie Pembroke

Harlequin Romance

Cinderellas in the Spotlight

Awakening His Shy Cinderella
A Midnight Kiss to Seal the Deal

A Fairytale Summer!

Italian Escape with Her Fake Fiancé

Road Trip with the Best Man
Carrying Her Millionaire's Baby
Pregnant on the Earl's Doorstep
Snowbound with the Heir
Second Chance for the Single Mom

Visit the Author Profile page
at Harlequin.com for more titles.

To Rachael Stewart, Andrea Bolter and Jessica Gilmore—my perfect matches! I've loved working with all of you on this series. Thank you for making it so much fun!

Praise for
Sophie Pembroke

CHAPTER ONE

Princess Isabella of Augusta turned her back on the huge, glass-fronted villa, eschewed the view from the decked terrace out over the beautiful Lake Geneva towards the Alps, and glared at her assistant, Gianna, instead.

'This is a bad idea.' Unthinkably bad. This was breaking rules that had been drummed into Isabella before she could even walk.

Gianna tossed her highlighted caramel hair over her shoulder. 'I don't have bad ideas.'

That was a blatant lie, as Isabella had met some of Gianna's ex-boyfriends when she'd brought them to the palace.

'You told me you were taking me to see Sofia.' Isabella's cousin, Sofia, would never dream of doing something so risky and ridiculous as this. Sofia followed The Rules.

Of course, The Rules had led to Sofia marrying the love of her life and living in the lap of luxury in Lake Geneva with her husband

and three adorable children, while also running her charity foundation for injured donkeys. The Rules hadn't been quite so kind to Isabella, but they had at least kept her safe and out of trouble.

This plan, she sensed, was a *lot* of trouble. Especially if her parents found out.

'This is better than another visit to Sofia,' Gianna said persuasively. 'This is a whole week of freedom, Your Highness. One week where you can be Bella for a change.'

'I'm always Bella with Sofia,' Isabella pointed out mulishly. She pushed away any thoughts of the one other person outside the royal family who'd been close enough to call her Bella, for a time. It would only make her miserable.

'*Sofia* thought it was a brilliant idea,' Gianna countered.

Isabella paused, blinked, and regrouped. 'Sofia *knows* about this plan?'

'Of course! Who do you think is covering for you if the King and Queen start asking any questions?'

It wouldn't be her parents, Their Royal Majesties King Leonardo and Queen Gabriela of Augusta, who'd be asking the questions, though, Isabella knew. It would be their private secretaries, or another member of household staff. Someone like Ferdinand, her father's right-hand man, whose job depended on all the royal children and cousins following The Rules.

His previous right-hand man had been fired after the last time Isabella thought there was a chance to break them. She'd been wrong, of course.

Just as Gianna was wrong now.

Isabella shook her head. 'Someone will find out.'

'They won't.' Pulling a folder from her laptop bag, Gianna spread out the papers on the high-gloss table in the middle of the terrace. She motioned for the Princess to take a seat and, dubiously, she did.

'Look.' Gianna pushed the top page towards her, and Isabella took in the stylised M of the logo, and the words 'discretion guaranteed' underneath. 'This isn't your usual dating agency, Your Highness. M only works with the rich and famous, and it offers them something they can't find anywhere else.'

'A villa on Lake Geneva?' Isabella said, knowing she was being facetious.

Gianna rolled her eyes, probably hoping her employer wasn't looking. '*Privacy.* They offer you one week with your perfect match in an ultra-exclusive, completely private and secluded location—they even arrange security, at a discreet distance.'

They were, Isabella had to admit, very much secluded. While the shores of Lake Geneva boasted many small towns and villages—as well as the city of Geneva itself—on both the Swiss and French sides of the border, it was large enough that villas, like the one Gianna had driven her to from the small private airfield where they'd landed, were miles away from any other signs of human habitation. Their nearest neighbour, as far as Isabella could see, was across the lake—far enough away that she could only make out the winking of sunlight on the windows of the building.

As for the rest of it…

'How could this agency possibly know my perfect match? Some sort of algorithm, I suppose, based on my star sign or my photograph?'

'No, not at all,' Gianna said patiently. 'You fill in an incredibly detailed personality test—'

'Which I didn't do,' Isabella pointed out.

'I did it for you.'

'Doesn't that rather defeat the point?'

Gianna gave her a long, steady look. 'Your Highness, I've been part of the palace since I was a child. I was your friend long before I was on your staff. I've seen you grow up, stifled by the court and their rules. I've seen *you*, all these years. Seen you cry. Seen you laugh. Seen you—'

She broke off there, but Isabella knew, instinctively, what her friend would have said. *Love*.

Gianna had been there the last time Isabella broke The Rules. She knew exactly what that had done to her.

If she wanted her to risk it again…there had to be a good reason.

'The point is, I know you,' Gianna went on. 'I know your hopes and your dreams, your loves and your hates. And I was willing to be honest about them on the form, which I know you wouldn't have been. You'd have been thinking about what the palace expected from you, what your parents wanted, what The Rules said. Anything except how you actually felt or what *you* wanted.'

'You're right,' Isabella admitted softly. 'I would have done that.' She pulled the brochure from M closer. 'It says here there's a video interview required, too? I didn't do one of those.'

'Yes, you did.' Gianna smiled wickedly. 'Remember that Internet chat you did with that website? The one for young women, seeking their place in the world?'

Isabella frowned. She didn't do many interviews or royal events these days, if she could

possibly avoid it. But Gianna had been insistent
about doing that particular one...

'The one with that woman? The pretty
one, from America? Morgan? No, Madison.
Madison Morgan, right?' She'd liked that interview. Madison Morgan had asked her all
sorts of interesting questions—much better
than the usual stuff she got asked in interviews like that. As the third child of the King
and Queen of Augusta she was a princess, but
she'd never rule the country—that was down to
her brother, Leo, named for their father. She'd
never had any real role beyond doing what she
was told. So all anyone really asked her was
who had designed her dress, and which parties
she'd be attending. The answer to the first was
usually, 'Ask Gianna,' and the second, 'None
if I can possibly avoid it.'

Morgan had asked her things about her*self.*
Who she was, who she wanted to be. What mattered to her most. What her ideal date looked
like... *How did I not see it?*

In fact, there *had* been a couple of moments that had struck her as odd during the
interview—questions that didn't quite make
sense, comments she didn't understand. At
the time, Isabella had put it down to cultural
differences, or her being out of practice at interviews, or even the language barrier. Her

English was fluent, and she was usually good at picking up idioms, but still, it wasn't her native tongue and that could cause problems sometimes. And there hadn't been anything to set alarm bells ringing—besides, Gianna had been there the whole time.

Of course, she had. Because she'd set this whole thing up.

'Why, Gianna?' Isabella asked now. 'Why did you do this?'

'Why did I risk my career and my future to find you a week of freedom and bliss with a man who might be your perfect match?' Gianna smiled, softly. 'Because you deserve it, Bella.'

How long since her best friend had last called her by that nickname? Too long. They'd become employer and employee, not friends, the moment Isabella reached adulthood.

Gianna took her hand. 'I've seen you, fake smiling through every date your family has arranged with a "suitable suitor". Every boring Augustian duke or lord, even the ones twenty years older than you. I've seen you miserable and lonely, because not everyone gets as lucky as Sofia did, and finds their perfect match in the palace. I've seen you trying to find a moment to just be you, away from the bodyguards or the cameras or the men who want to marry into the royal family. I've seen you withering away in that palace ever since Nathanial—'

'Don't.' Isabella shook her head violently. 'Not…just, don't.'

'Okay. Okay.' Gianna ran her fingers soothingly over the Princess's arm. 'But you were miserable, Your Highness. And I saw something I could do about that…so I did it.'

'Do you really think this will change anything?' Isabella met her friend's gaze with her own, and found nothing but compassion there. 'One week with some guy? It's not like he's going to magically turn out to be a mysterious aristocrat or something. He won't be someone my parents would let me marry—I've already met every single guy they consider suitable. So it can't ever be more than this—just one week with someone I *might* be…compatible with.'

She felt a slight heat rise in her cheeks as she said the words. She hadn't been *compatible* with anyone for a very long time. Just once, in fact. With Na— No. She wasn't even going to think his name.

Did Gianna really think that a week with a man some agency thought was her perfect match would fix everything that was wrong with Isabella?

'Maybe it won't change *everything*,' Gianna admitted. 'But it might help. At worst, it's a week of fun and freedom—no bodyguards, except Tessa from your staff, and the small security team the agency sent to guard the perimeter, and they'll all be at the cabin on the edge of the estate. No royal obligations, no expectations. Just a guy that you might like…and the chance to have some fun, if you want it.'

'I'm not looking for that, either,' Isabella said flatly. How could she? *That* was definitely against The Rules.

Gianna sighed. 'Bella, this isn't some sort of hook-up agency I went to here. It's M. The premier, most expensive and exclusive dating agency in the business. Whoever they've sent to meet you, he's not here for sex. He's here to get to know you.'

The knot in Isabella's stomach started to loosen, just a little. 'You're sure?' Maybe she could come out of this having made a friend. A friend would be nice. A lover would be… trouble. Lots of trouble.

'Sure.' Gianna glanced over Isabella's shoulder, then gave her a mischievous grin. 'But looking at your Perfect Match, you might want to consider just a *little* romance this week.'

Isabella's heart thudded in her chest as she realised she *wanted* that. She wanted to find someone to talk with, relax with, laugh with, even love with, in a way she'd hadn't in so long. In a way she'd stopped hoping for.

But what was the point, if it was only for one week?

She shook her head. 'No, Gianna. A friend is one thing. Anything else is—'

'Against The Rules,' her friend finished for her, rolling her eyes.

'Yes.' But it wasn't just The Rules, Isabella realised. It was the risk. To her reputation, her family…her heart. She'd risked it all for love once before. It wasn't a mistake she intended to make again.

Gianna was still staring blatantly at the glass-fronted villa where Isabella's perfect match was waiting. If she wanted this week away from reality, Isabella knew she had to turn now. Had to see what sort of person M had decided was right for her. Had to open up her mind and her heart to the possibility of a friendship beyond The Rules.

Sucking in a deep breath, Isabella turned slowly to face the villa on the lake, and stared up through the glass to the man standing, one hand on his hip, the other holding a phone to his ear, looking down at them from what had to be the bedroom.

Was he really so tall, or was it just because she was looking up at him? Either way, the glass and the distance between them couldn't hide his admirable figure—the breadth of his shoulders, the muscles showing through the tight T-shirt he wore, or the long legs with their thick thighs… His black hair was cropped short, his skin as tanned and warm as her own Mediterranean complexion.

He was, she had to admit, the best-looking man she'd ever been set up on a date with. But then, the bar for that had never been particularly high.

Most of all, though, he looked like trouble.

He looked down, and her breath caught in her chest as his gaze met hers.

Maybe Madison knows what she's doing, she thought as the funny feeling in her chest moved lower, turning warmer. Maybe this guy wasn't her perfect match, but she couldn't deny the heat she felt at the idea of a week alone with him.

She pushed it aside. A new friend, that was what she was looking for here.

Even if that new friend looked like sin and risk and everything she'd spent every moment since Nathanial avoiding. She couldn't imagine what M thought they'd have in common, but she supposed there must be something. As Gianna said, they'd been matched on their personalities, first and foremost.

'So, you're going in?' Gianna asked, a giggle in her voice.

Isabella swallowed. 'Well, I've come this far.' She'd already left all but one of her security staff at the airport, lied to her parents about where she was, and apparently dragged Sofia in on the deception. 'What's one week?'

One small risk—a week away, getting to know a new friend. After that, she'd go back to The Rules. She'd be Princess Isabella again, and everything that entailed.

But first, she'd have this one week of freedom.

With him.

Matteo Rossi stared out over Lake Geneva through the huge panes of glass that spanned the whole front of the villa. It was quite the view, he had to admit that. The lake glistening in the late-afternoon sun, the snow-peaked mountains in the distance, even in June. And it was definitely in the middle of nowhere— which he was pretty sure his management team had insisted on. Nowhere for him to get into trouble, and wasn't that the whole point of this week?

'So, it's nice?' his manager, Gabe, asked on the other end of the phone line, probably happily ensconced in his office in Rome, preparing for the next race. A race where Matteo pointedly *wasn't* driving, even though his broken leg had healed perfectly well already. 'Madison promised it would be nice.'

Ah, yes, the famous Madison Morgan. Former child actress and now the owner of the M dating agency, the latest strategy Gabe and the others had hit on to slow him down, and the reason he was now stuck in Switzerland and not on the racetrack where he belonged.

'It's fine,' Matteo said dismissively. He'd stayed in some of the finest hotels in the world, from Abu Dhabi to Las Vegas and home to Rome. This villa was just a building, impressive though it was.

'And is *she* there yet?' There was a knowing lilt in Gabe's voice, a teasing note. Because Gabe wasn't talking about Madison, of course.

He was talking about Matteo's Perfect Match.

Matteo rolled his eyes just thinking the words.

'No, she's not here yet.' But then he looked down at the terrace outside the villa and saw two women talking. One—with caramel hair and a skirt suit—was obviously talking a mile a minute, if the way her hands were waving around was anything to go by. She was pretty, Matteo conceded. But his attention was already held by the other woman, the one with her back to him.

Dark curls tumbled down her back, loose and wild, falling almost to where her waist nipped in before curving out over generous hips. From what he could tell from behind, she had her arms folded in front of her, one hip tilted out as she stood, as if she was listening to what her companion had to say but didn't really believe it.

Her. He felt the word run through his body more than he consciously thought it, but he knew in an instant it was true. If she wasn't the woman Madison had picked for his perfect match, then the woman was doing her job wrong.

Suddenly, the idea of this week in exile wasn't looking quite so bad.

Except, no. Because whichever woman was here to meet him, she'd be expecting something he couldn't give. The M agency didn't do booty calls; his perfect match was expecting true love. Commitment. Forever.

Matteo had far too many adventures in his future to even *think* about settling down with someone. Which meant he couldn't give the woman the wrong idea.

Still, they'd been matched on personality, so hopefully hanging out with her for a week wouldn't be too bad. They could blow this place and go explore the region. There had to be *some* interesting things to do around here, and, if she was his perfect match, she'd be up for an adventure.

Just as long as he made it clear she couldn't expect anything more.

'Are you looking forward to meeting her?' Gabe asked. Was it just guilt keeping his manager on the line so long? He'd sent Matteo here, away from his team, away from racing. They'd told him it was for his own good—a treat, even. But Matteo knew the truth.

This was a last-ditch attempt to repair his reputation—and his sponsorship deals. Apparently some of his most recent adventures had cut a bit too close to the line. Were they hoping that the lure of true love would tame him? Stop him chasing after the next adventure, taking bigger risk after bigger risk?

If they were, they were going to be disappointed.

'I guess,' he replied. After all, he wanted to save those sponsorship deals, too. Not to mention his career. He'd already made more money than he could spend in a lifetime, on and off the track. But if he didn't have racing, his dream career, what would he do?

Whose dream career? The whispered question in the back of his mind surprised him.

See, this was what happened when he slowed down. He started thinking. And unless he was thinking about speed and angles and winning, what was the point? As a rule, Matteo getting all introspective wasn't good for anybody. He acted, that was who he was. Who he'd always been.

Only since Giovanni died.

That voice. Matteo shook it away and turned his attention back to the women by the lake instead. Women, he understood. The thoughts that came to him late at night, or when he wasn't distracted by something fun...those he didn't *want* to understand.

But as he looked down, he realised the woman with the dark hair, his possible perfect match, had turned around to face him. Even through the glass, and over the distance between them, he felt it the moment her gaze met his. A feeling that hit his chest and spread through his body. And he wasn't entirely sure he understood that, either.

It was just her curves, he told himself. The way her folded arms highlighted her perfect breasts, the narrowness of her waist and the arch of her hips. Or her mouth, full and luscious. A purely physical reaction to a beautiful woman, nothing more. Of course, it was.

'It's just one week, Matteo,' Gabe was saying, when he finally tuned back into the phone conversation. 'Just…stay out of trouble this week. Finish healing.'

'My leg—'

'I know, I know. The doctors said it was fine, but they also said not to push it too far, too soon. And that's basically your motto in life, so…just take the week. When you get back, we'll come up with the next stage of the plan to get you back out on the racetrack. But, Matteo?'

There was something in his manager's voice that made him nervous. 'Yeah?'

'If you *did* happen to come out of this week happy, in love and ready to settle down with the love of your life… I don't think any of your sponsors would be disappointed.'

Because as much as they wanted the maverick, risky moves that won races, they needed him to appear a good role model for the younger fans, responsible enough that people trusted the things he was selling, however tangentially.

How do they expect me to be a champion and *a boring, stay-at-home guy, all at the same time?* The adrenaline was in his blood. The need to live life to the fullest, to chase every dream, tackle every challenge, beat every odd—on the track and off.

Except, the last time he'd gone adventuring, the odds had beaten him. Calling Gabe from the hospital to admit that he'd broken his leg while cliff diving, two weeks before the Dutch Grand Prix, had not been his finest moment.

Everyone wanted him to slow down—just not when he was behind the wheel.

Matteo sighed. 'Message received.' He hung up.

Down below, the terrace was empty—and he heard the electric buzz of the front door closing and locking behind whoever had just keyed in the confidential code. A code only he and the woman who was supposed to be his perfect match had.

No sign of the other woman outside, either, so he couldn't know exactly who was waiting for him downstairs—he just hoped he was right in his guess.

He didn't believe for a moment that some agency could find him his dream woman based on a questionnaire—one he'd been forced to fill in while still in the hospital—or a brief video interview, which he'd done with his leg in plaster, propped up on Gabe's coffee table.

But if the right woman was waiting downstairs—if she really was a match for his restless, reckless spirit—they might at least have found a way to stop him thinking too much. And Matteo would take that as good enough for now.

CHAPTER TWO

IT WASN'T UNTIL the door swung shut behind her, the alarm beeped, and the sound of Gianna's car driving away down that long, private driveway faded, that Isabella realised this could be a massive mistake.

She was alone in a house in the middle of nowhere with a man she'd never met. Sure, Gianna said there were security personnel in the cabin down the driveway—including Isabella's own long-term security woman, Tessa, apparently—towards the perimeter of the grounds, but what if she was wrong? What if this was a set-up? What if Gianna had been blackmailed into bringing her here? What if…?

No. Gianna never would—not for anything. One betrayal didn't mean Isabella had to keep looking for another one around every corner, and, besides, she was a very minor royal of a very minor Mediterranean country. Nobody would go to this much trouble to set her up, would they?

Isabella forced herself to breathe slowly, mindfully, as she took in her surroundings. Modern, sparse furnishings—the opposite of the palace at Augusta with all its heavy wood and dark antiques. Bright white walls, and comfortable-looking sofas loaded with cushions and blankets in various textures and shades of white, both looking out over Lake Geneva. She supposed the interior designer who furnished the place hadn't wanted anything to distract from that incredible view, through that all-glass wall out to the water.

She felt calmer already. This villa might not be like anywhere she'd stayed before—her family tended towards the traditional, even when travelling—but there was something about it. Something peaceful.

Hopeful, even.

This place gave her hope that she might be able to take this week to regroup, to find herself again after so long feeling adrift in her royal world.

Following The Rules was all well and good, and after everything with Nathanial she understood better than ever why it was important. But still, she couldn't help feeling hemmed in sometimes. As if she were pushing against tightly woven walls of cloth holding her in, stopping her from stretching, from reaching out for something more.

Maybe here, in peace and solitude, she could figure out what that something more was.

Except she wasn't alone, was she?

She heard a tread on the stairs behind her and knew it must be him. Her perfect match, if such a thing really existed.

She hoped he wasn't dreaming of too much from this week. A fairy-tale ending with a princess, for instance. Because however nice he was, that wasn't in her power to give. Friendship was all she had to offer.

Pasting on a smile, Isabella turned away from the lake to face him.

Gosh, he was even better looking up close. That cropped black hair, curling tightly against his skull. Those bright green eyes. And that body...tall, lean but obviously muscled; she'd been able to tell that even from a distance. Up close it was almost overwhelming, the sheer physicality of him.

He was staring at her, too. Good. At least she didn't have to worry about being accused of ogling. She wondered what he saw. Did he know who she was? Probably not, unless Madison had told him; she wasn't exactly highly visible outside Augusta, most of the time, and the palace had been keeping an even tighter rein than normal over her publicity since the incident five years ago.

Isabella frowned. Should she know who *he* was? He looked faintly familiar, in some way, but she couldn't put her finger on it. And it wasn't as if she were particularly well up on the rich, famous and notable of Europe—or the world—either. Since her father mostly just involved her brother Leo in international business, the only men she really got to meet were potential suitors. Especially since Nate.

And none of her suitors had *ever* looked like this man.

'Hi,' he said, finally, a wide, open smile spreading across his face. 'I'm Matteo. Matteo Rossi.'

Even the name rang a bell, but she still couldn't tell from where.

She moved forward to meet him as he descended the last few steps, and held out her hand. 'Isabella.' And then, because there was no point trying to hide these things, she continued, 'Princess Isabella of Augusta.'

Matteo's eyebrows shot up and, instead of shaking her hand as he'd clearly been about to, he twisted it and brought it to his lips. 'Should I bow?' he murmured as he kissed the backs of her fingers.

He should, really, she supposed. But the warmth that spread through her from the touch of his lips on her skin was more than an adequate substitute.

'It's probably going to get a little awkward if you have to go around the house bowing to me all week,' she said, after pretending to consider it for a moment. 'I think we can let it go, just this once. Under the circumstances.'

Matteo straightened up and stepped back, but kept a hold of her hand, a wicked smile dancing over his lips. 'Good to know, Your Highness.'

'Isabella, please.' Maybe she didn't want to be a princess this week. Not with this man.

Maybe she wanted to be something more than just royal. Human, perhaps.

'Ah, but I'm only a humble racing-car driver, Your Highness,' he teased. 'Are you sure it would be appropriate?'

'*That's* where I've seen you before!' Isabella snapped her fingers as it came to her. Humble racing-car driver her foot. Even *she* knew that he'd made the rich list last year, his billions earned from racing and sponsorship deals ratcheting him up the rankings. 'Matteo Rossi. I watched you race in Barcelona last year. You won, of course.'

That had been a treat for her. A rare trip out of Augusta with Leo and his wife. A chance to escape the stifling air of the palace, just for a few days. She hadn't seen much of Barcelona, but watching the cars racing around the track she'd envied them their freedom. Until her sister-in-law, Princess Serena, had pointed out that they only ever went in circles, and only where someone else pointed them.

Isabella had wondered if maybe *nobody* had the kind of freedom she dreamed of sometimes, late at night, with the windows open. But looking at the man in front of her now…he didn't seem hemmed in by anybody.

She would bet he could go anywhere, any time, with anybody, whenever he chose.

And he was here in Lake Geneva with her.

A nervous excitement jolted through her at the realisation. Maybe she could learn a little freedom from this man. And she had a feeling she would enjoy the lesson.

A princess. Madison Morgan thought his dream woman was a freaking *princess*?

Matteo hadn't exactly spent time memorising the names and faces of European nobility, but he was still surprised he hadn't recognised her. Hell, she'd recognised *him*, and he was nobody, really.

Well, he was the world champion, but what

did that really mean to people who didn't follow the sport? What did it mean to *royalty*?

He was still holding her hand. He should stop that.

He'd been so relieved when he'd walked down the stairs to find the curvaceous, dark-haired woman standing with her back to him again, looking out over the lake. The idea that she might have left before he found out if that instant connection he'd felt when their gazes had met meant something had been unbearable to him.

Now, he wasn't sure what any of it meant. The Princess seemed…cautious. Guarded, perhaps. There was something in her eyes, even when she was joking about him bowing, that told him this was not a woman who let people in. Which was okay by him, since he didn't particularly want or need anyone getting close to him, either.

But a princess. He was pretty sure she'd never climbed Machu Picchu or been bungee jumping or travelled across America in a convertible, as he'd done over the past few years. From her tone when she talked about watching him race in Barcelona, he suspected that was the most excitement she'd had in years. Just *watching* someone else have fun.

That was what royals did, wasn't it? They hid

away in their palaces and watched over other people actually living their lives.

Which begged the question, what was a princess doing signing up to an exclusive dating service? Let alone spending a week in a secluded location with a strange man, like him. She couldn't really believe *he* could be her perfect match, could she? And if she did, he needed to disabuse her of that idea pretty quick.

More than ever, he was glad he'd already resolved that this week would be about friendship and fun, rather than romance or anything more. He liked a risk as much as the next guy, but he *definitely* wasn't Prince Charming material.

Somewhere behind him, something pinged. And then it did it again.

'Is that…some sort of security alarm?' Isabella asked, her eyebrows furrowed.

Matteo listened to the ping. 'I think it's an oven timer, actually.'

Even a place as designer and minimalist as this villa on the lake had to have a kitchen, right? And it sounded as if someone had planned dinner for them.

'Come on, Princess. Let's go investigate.'

Downstairs had seemed completely open plan—with sitting areas and a dining table and a well-stocked bar with stools, all looking out towards the incredible view. But first appearances could be deceiving, Matteo realised. Behind the white stone staircase that ran from the centre of the room up to the first floor was a hidden corridor—one that led to a state-of-the-art kitchen, and a pinging oven timer.

With a little trial and error, Matteo found the right button to stop it pinging, turned down the oven temperature and opened the door. There were oven gloves hanging right next to it, and he used them to lift out a steaming dish of lasagne. His mouth watered at the sight. This was *proper* food.

Normally, when he was training, he watched his diet carefully to keep himself at peak fitness. Everything made a difference on the track and, besides, he was usually training for something else as well—like the Machu Picchu hike, or the Paris marathon, or a cross-Channel swim.

While he'd been in recovery with his broken leg, he'd kept up the habits—keen to show the team that he was ready to get back out there the moment it was healed. But since he'd been sidelined anyway, sent to Lake Geneva to keep him out of trouble…surely a little lasagne wouldn't hurt.

He turned and placed the dish on a waiting trivet on the marble counter, and found two plates already set out with fresh salad, complete with gleaming red tomatoes, and the gloss of oil and balsamic vinegar. A marble bowl filled with crusty bread sat beside it. Matteo touched it; still warm.

'That door must lead to the housekeeper's quarters,' he guessed, nodding towards a slim white door, almost camouflaged between the kitchen cabinets. '"Discreet household staff included,"' he quoted from M's literature.

'It looks delicious.' Isabella's eyes had lit up at the sight of the food. He supposed having actual staff would just be commonplace for her, growing up in a palace. But for him, even since he'd reached the heights of his career and grown more or less accustomed to having staff and help around for the day-to-day essentials of life, it still felt like an incredible luxury.

If Giovanni could see me now. On holiday with a princess, with staff *to do all the cooking and cleaning.*

His brother wouldn't believe it. Not even in his wildest dreams. Not after their childhood in Rome, both taking on their share of the household tasks while their mother worked two jobs to keep a roof over their heads.

But Giovanni couldn't see him, and neither could his mother. Or if, as Matteo sometimes let himself hope, they could look down from above and watch him, they couldn't tell him what they thought of his lifestyle—his success, his billions in the bank, his fame.

Sometimes, he wished they could, so he could hear their advice. Other times, he thought it was just as well they couldn't. He could only imagine the bickering.

'There was a table out on the balcony upstairs,' he said impulsively as he dished up the lasagne onto the waiting plates. 'Why don't we take it up there to eat?'

Isabella nodded and, between them, they loaded up a couple of trays with the food and cutlery, as well as the carafe of wine and the glasses that had been laid out for them. Negotiating the stairs slowly, Matteo made a joke about not dropping anything on these stone floors and was gratified when Isabella laughed.

He wasn't sure what he'd expected when she'd said the word 'princess', but this pasta-loving beauty wasn't exactly it.

He heard her falter behind him, though, as he reached the bedroom. Placing his tray down on the table on the balcony, he turned back to find her staring at the bed.

'There's another bedroom next door,' he told her, quickly realising the cause of her alarm. 'I thought I could use that one, if you wanted to be in here? I think the staff have already brought up our bags.'

Her gaze flickered from the bed to the solitary suitcase beside it—her suitcase, he assumed, since he'd already put his next door. Who knew how the staff had managed that without them noticing.

The view was just as good from both rooms, he'd decided, and the balcony here stretched between the two rooms anyway, accessible from either one of the glass doors that were in place in lieu of windows or walls, over the lake.

'Oh, okay. Great.' Her stretched smile didn't look quite natural, though. Matteo tried to look reassuring as he reached over to take the wine and glasses from her.

Of course, she still thought this week was about romance and love—and sex. Whereas he'd already known that true love wasn't on the cards for him, even before the discovery that she was a princess. They were worlds apart in so many ways—but she'd come here under a false assumption. That he was looking for love.

He needed to set that straight.

Pouring a glass of wine for them both, Matteo waited for Isabella to take her seat at the small balcony table before sitting down himself. His mother had instilled *some* manners in him, at least.

Then he waited until she'd taken a large mouthful of lasagne—so she'd have time to think about her answer—then asked his question.

'So, what's a princess doing using an elite dating site? Don't you have to marry a prince or something?'

The food—delicious as it was—turned to ashes in her mouth at Matteo's question.

Don't you have to marry a prince?

He'd put his finger straight on the biggest problem with this whole set-up. She wasn't free to fall in love with whoever M decided her perfect match was. And she needed to tell him that.

'Not necessarily a prince,' she said, with a small, one-shoulder shrug. 'But a lord or a duke, yeah. Preferably Augustian, to make my father *really* happy.'

'Are there many Augustian lords and dukes your age?'

'I think my cousin married the last of them.' She didn't begrudge Sofia her happiness—or her husband. But it did narrow the acceptable dating pool quite considerably.

'Ah. So that's why you're here?' Matteo grinned. 'Because I think you already know I'm not a duke or a lord.'

No. He was a *racing-car driver,* of all things. Isabella could just imagine her brother's face if he knew where she was right now, who she was with. Leo sometimes seemed even more hide-bound and determined to follow The Rules—or, at least, make Isabella follow them—than the King and Queen were.

For a man who was supposed to be her perfect match, it was hard to think of anyone less suitable. From what she knew of his reputation—which was mostly stuff she'd heard whispered in the crowd in Barcelona last year—he was a risk-taker, a daredevil. A Lothario on the racing circuit.

The absolute opposite to the stuffed-shirt lords her parents had been setting her up on dates with for the last five years.

But if he realised she wasn't really his perfect match, he didn't seem too disappointed.

Isabella reached for a piece of bread and dipped it in the waiting oil and vinegar. Her mother, if she were here, would have looked despairingly at Isabella's hips. But she wasn't here—nobody was, except Matteo—so it was safe to be a little bit rebellious, right? *Ooh, look at you, eating bread. You rebel.*

And having dinner with a racing-car driver. That probably counted more.

'I'm here because my assistant, Gianna, lied to me,' she said casually, as if things like this happened to her all the time.

Matteo sat back in his seat, eyebrows high,

his arms folded across his chest. 'She told you that you were meeting a prince?'

'She told me I was going to visit my cousin for the week, like I often do at this time of year. That's what she told the palace, and my parents, too. Nobody knows I'm here except for Gianna, my cousin Sofia, Tessa—the longest serving and most trusted member of my security team, Madison Morgan—and you.' It felt dangerous, giving up that secret. Information that could hurt her, if Matteo chose to share it with the papers, or via the internet.

But it felt good, too. Freeing.

What was that quote? Publish and be damned. But she didn't think that Matteo would suddenly jump on social media and reveal her whereabouts. After all, discretion was guaranteed by the M dating agency, and she couldn't imagine Madison Morgan would be very happy with him—or give him another chance to find his one true love—if he broke that rule.

Which brought her back to her original problem. Matteo was there to find his perfect match. That was who he was expecting to meet when he walked into the villa. And instead he got her—a princess who couldn't fall in love with him even if she wanted to, and had now admitted she was only there because she was tricked into it.

She must be quite a disappointment to him.

It was probably a good job she was used to being a disappointment to people.

'I'm sorry,' she said. 'You came here to find your perfect match, and it's only the first night and I've already ruined that for you.' She got to her feet. 'This wasn't fair. Let me call Madison and explain, and I'm sure she'll refund you, or find you an *actual* perfect match for your next date.'

Matteo laughed, and Isabella paused half out of her chair, unsure what was funny about the situation.

'I'm not laughing at you,' he said after a moment, obviously sensing her discomfort. She was a princess. She really wasn't used to people laughing at her—well, apart from her older siblings, of course. Leo and Rosa could always find *something* hilarious about her words or actions—when they weren't being horrified.

He motioned for her to sit back down, and she did so cautiously. But there was still lasagne and bread left—she assumed the meal had been planned towards his cultural heritage, and wondered whether tomorrow might bring an Augustian speciality, or even a Swiss one—and she hated to leave good food uneaten.

'So why *are* you laughing?' she asked, reaching for another piece of the delicious, still-warm bread.

'Because this whole situation is hilarious.' Matteo leaned across the table, closer to her than anyone who wasn't an employee or a blood relative had been in a very long time. Then, swiping the last piece of bread from the bowl, he said, 'You see, I didn't choose to come here either.'

Isabella blinked. 'You…didn't?' He was already sitting back in his chair, smirking at her as he chewed his prize, but she could still feel his breath against her cheek as he spoke.

What was it about this man that affected her so? Was it just that it had been such a long time since she'd found a man attractive at all? Now, sitting across the table from Matteo Rossi, with all that lean, long muscle and that smirk… Isabella admitted to herself that it had *definitely* been too long.

Not that she could really do anything about that, unless she wanted to marry one of the stuffed shirts Leo kept setting her up with.

Back to the point. 'So, why are you here?'

This was supposed to be their perfect date, their chance to find true love—without the usual scrutiny of the press or the public. But if *neither* of them had chosen to be there at all, where did that leave them?

'Same reason as you, more or less.' With a shrug, Matteo reached over for the carafe of red wine and topped up her glass. 'My management team thought it was a good idea.'

'Why?' Isabella thought she understood why Gianna believed it was a good idea for her to be there—a chance to kick back, relax, have the freedom to be herself, and maybe even have some fun. But surely Matteo had all those things available to him in the real world, in a way that the Princess of Augusta really didn't.

'To keep me out of trouble.' One eyebrow arched up above Matteo's bright green eyes. 'Although we might be able to find just a *little* bit of trouble here this week, don't you think?'

And from the heat that pulsed through her body at his words, Isabella had to agree.

This man could be an awful lot of trouble.

CHAPTER THREE

HER EYES DARKENED at his words; he could see it, clear as day in the fading evening light.

But he couldn't do anything about it.

She's a princess, Matteo. It was his mother's voice in his head, even after all these years. *Have some respect.*

Yeah, he was pretty sure Gabe and the sponsors wouldn't have sent him here if they'd known who his perfect match was. They'd be too afraid of his causing an international incident or something.

Matteo wasn't entirely sure it wasn't a possibility himself.

He looked away, turning his attention back to the bread in his hand as if it were the most fascinating thing on the balcony, and added, 'I mean, if you're my perfect match, you must like a little adventure, right? There have to be places to explore around here…'

He trailed off as he saw her eyes widen in

horror. Yeah, his first instincts hadn't been wrong. The Princess wasn't a risk-taker.

'Or we could hang out here at the villa, get to know one another,' he finished with a sigh.

Isabella visibly relaxed, her eyes lighting up. 'That sounds nice. It's not often I get the opportunity to make a new friend.'

He couldn't help but return her smile. It might not be the week he'd plan for himself, but he got the impression that the Princess needed to be gentled along in this. By the end of the week, he was sure he'd manage to talk her into *some* small adventure.

'So if you were tricked into coming here, what made you stay?' Matteo asked, curious.

Isabella looked up and met his gaze with her own, direct, brown one. And just as it had when she'd looked up at him in the window of the villa earlier, his chest tightened.

For a moment, he was almost certain she was going to say, *You.*

She didn't, and he tried not to feel disappointed at that.

'At the palace my life is rather…let's say tightly controlled.'

'You mean boring?' he guessed.

That raised half a smile from her. 'Amongst other things. And I decided that a week away from that—a week to relax and be myself, not just Princess Isabella—might be good for me. Plus,' she added, with an impish grin that lit up her whole face, 'I was pretty sure from the moment I saw you that the last thing you'd be was boring. And that was before I even realised you were a racing star!'

No, Matteo had never been accused of being boring. At least, not since Giovanni died, and he started living his life for both of them.

'So, you're looking for someone to help you relax and have a bit of fun for a change, then, rather than your true love?' That worked out nicely for him, even if her idea of adventure didn't match his.

'I guess I am.' Isabella sounded almost surprised at her own words, as if she hadn't really factored him into her plans, despite what she'd said about him not being boring. 'What about you? What are you looking for out of this week, if it's not your perfect match?'

What *was* he looking for?

'Well, like I said, my management team are just hoping to keep me out of trouble.'

Isabella raised her eyebrows at that. 'Seems kind of an extreme way of doing it—going through all the rigmarole of setting you up with the M agency. It's not exactly cheap, either, from what I understand.'

'One hundred grand deposit,' Matteo agreed

with a wince. Even now that amount was a tiny drop in his investment and savings accounts, he still couldn't help but imagine his mother's horror at the casual way he spent it. 'But at least most of it goes to charity.' He'd donated his chunk to the cancer charity he'd supported ever since they'd helped Giovanni through those last weeks and days. That way, something good was coming out of his side-lining, he'd reasoned.

Isabella gave a low whistle, which seemed kind of out of keeping for a princess. But then, he was coming to suspect that she wasn't just any princess. 'You must have *really* got in a lot of trouble for them to go that far. What did you do?'

'Broke my leg cliff diving,' he admitted, and she winced.

'Ouch. It's better now?'

'Yeah. Docs all say it should be as good as new.' Even if it still ached a little, most days. He was doing his strengthening exercises, and he sure as hell wouldn't let it affect his driving. That was what mattered. 'But I was out of commission for a while. Couldn't race, couldn't work out, couldn't do anything much.'

He'd hated that—the inaction—more than anything. That was still one of the concerns he had about this week. If she expected him to sit around doing nothing…he'd end up abseiling down from the roof out of sheer boredom.

'It wasn't just the broken leg, though,' he admitted. 'I guess the team—and Gabe, my manager, in particular—were fed up with my antics in general.' In fact, he knew they were, because those were the exact words Gabe had used at the team intervention. He'd been lying there in his hospital bed, lucky to be alive, and Gabe had been ranting about 'your antics putting everything at risk'.

He'd apologised later, although Matteo hadn't needed him to. He knew what fear and love sounded like together, and Gabe had been like an older brother to him since he'd lost his own.

'You're a bit of a daredevil, huh?' Isabella asked.

Matteo shrugged. 'You could say that. I like adventures.' It sounded easy, when he said it like that. The truth was more complicated, of course, but wasn't it always? And in his experience, girls didn't want to hear the truth. They wanted the story, the fairy tale of the wild and reckless racing-car driver. Even if behaving that way on the track would only get people killed. Matteo was always responsible behind the wheel, even if no one watching would ever see that.

And that was the problem. The public—and

the sponsors—only saw him speeding around corners at work, then taking risks in his private life. His reputation was established—and it wasn't the sort of reputation that got him respect.

'And now you're stuck here with me for a week, in a luxury villa with excellent food.' Isabella polished off the last of the wine in her glass and glanced over at the desserts still sitting on the tray.

'Pudding?' Matteo suggested and she nodded enthusiastically. The Princess liked her food. Matteo made a mental note in case that came in useful some time.

He got the feeling he was going to get to know a lot about the Princess this week. And he found himself strangely thrilled at the idea.

Maybe *she* was his next adventure after all.

Isabella had expected to struggle to sleep in a strange place, but the bed in the villa was so comfortable, and the food, wine and company over dinner had been so pleasant, that she found herself sleeping in the next morning.

By the time she woke, the sun was already high above the lake, streaming through the gauzy curtains that covered the floor-to-ceiling windows—and she could hear the sound of coffee cups on the balcony.

Coffee. That sounded like something worth getting up for.

Dragging herself out of bed, she wrapped her dressing gown around her, blushing as she realised what Gianna considered appropriate nightwear for a princess on holiday wasn't exactly modest. Her pale pink silk pyjama shorts and matching camisole were barely covered by the thin, short white broderie wrap.

She paused for a second by the glass doors to the balcony. Maybe she should shower and dress before heading out. But the coffee smelled so good…

'If you don't get out here quick, I'm going to eat all the pastries,' Matteo called from outside. 'I'm starving.'

Well, that made the decision for her. There was no way she was missing out on pastries.

Matteo was already sitting at the table they'd shared the night before—at some point in the night, it must have been cleared and reset, as it was now laden with pastries and steaming hot coffee. Isabella looked around and spotted a small staircase she'd missed the previous night, leading down to where she imagined the kitchen door must be at the side of the house. Whoever their house fairies were, sent to take care of them this week, they were certainly discreet and silent.

Taking a breath, Isabella stepped forward, her princess smile in place, and took her seat opposite him. 'Good morning.'

His eyes widened as he looked up and clocked her nightwear, but he didn't say anything, which she appreciated. And he poured her coffee, which she appreciated even more.

'Have you been up long?' She took the cup and lifted it to her lips, breathing in the bitter scent and taking one cautious, hot sip.

Matteo shrugged. 'A little while. Went for an early morning run by the lake, then came back for a shower. When I came out, I found breakfast ready.'

'You still run on holiday?' Exercise for Isabella was limited to yoga classes with Gianna, and walks around the palace estates.

'It's a habit,' he replied. 'Plus I'm still strengthening my leg. The physio gave me exercises, but now it's more about rebuilding my stamina.'

'I wouldn't have thought that driving was a particularly fitness-focused sport.' Although given the way his muscles showed through his thin white T-shirt—dampened in places from the water dripping from his tight black curls— she wasn't really surprised to learn that he took his physical fitness seriously.

'I hear that a lot.' Matteo leant back in his

chair, one foot propped up on his other knee, his arm sprawled across the railing on the edge of the balcony. Just looking at him made her cheeks feel warm at her suggestion. *Of course* he was in peak physical condition. 'Actually, fitness is really important in racing.'

At least he didn't seem annoyed by her comment. 'How come?'

'Well, first off there's the strength needed for controlling the car at high speeds.' Matteo ticked that point off on his finger before raising another one. 'There's the heat to contend with in there, too. But most of all, it's our hearts.'

'Your heart?'

'A race can be two hours long,' Matteo explained. 'And our hearts are pumping at way above normal levels for that whole time—like we're exercising hard for a sustained period. The G-forces over a two-hour race are immense—you feel like your head weighs ten times what it normally does.'

'I hadn't thought about any of that,' Isabella admitted.

'No reason you should,' he replied, with a shrug. 'For me, the biggest thing is my brain.'

'Yeah?' She also hadn't really thought of racing as a particularly cerebral activity either, but she figured it probably wasn't a good idea to mention that.

'Racing needs split-second reactions, it needs me to be able to think ahead, to calculate risks and take them quickly. If my body is tired, my brain gets tired too and my concentration starts to lapse. I can't afford that in a race; it could cost me too much.'

Not just the winner's flag, Isabella realised. If Matteo lost focus out of the racetrack, if he wasn't up to the rigours of a two-hour race, it could cost him—or someone else—their life. She shivered, even though the morning was warm.

He seemed to sense her discomfort with the topic and moved on.

'So, what do you have planned for today?' Matteo topped up her almost empty cup of coffee and she took it gratefully, sipping the hot liquid carefully while she considered her answer.

Planned? She didn't have anything planned. There was no Gianna standing there with her schedule for the day, reminding her of appearances she'd reluctantly agreed to make, or letters she needed to write. No member of the royal household summoning her for another awful, awkward date with a man she didn't want to marry. No rules keeping her from escaping into the city and exploring alone. No security guard trailing after her, even—although she suspected that if she tried to pass the gatehouse where the security staff were staying, she'd soon pick one up.

The point was, there was nothing she was *supposed* to be doing today. Which meant she could choose for herself.

What a luxury.

And a pity she had no idea what to do with it.

'I saw a well-stocked bookcase inside,' she said eventually. 'Maybe I'll read.'

'Sounds good,' Matteo replied, not really sounding as if he meant it.

She supposed that was a little antisocial, considering she was supposed to be getting to know her companion better. 'There were some board games too, I think?'

A wide smile spread across Matteo's face. 'Now, that sounds more like it. But I warn you—I'm very competitive.'

'Why am I not surprised?' Isabella asked, grinning in return.

By later that afternoon, Matteo was regretting almost everything about this week.

Well, that wasn't strictly true. Mostly, he was just regretting his personal promise to himself to keep his hands off the Princess.

From the moment she'd appeared that morning, dressed in those indecently short pyjamas and a wrap that was basically see-through, he'd been struggling to keep his eyes—and his libido—where they belonged.

He'd thought that playing board games would help. After all, he associated them with being a kid, playing with his brother. They were inherently unsexy, and she'd even put real clothes on to play them. It was the perfect 'new friend' activity, right?

Except it turned out that Princess Isabella had a competitive streak to rival his own, and the wicked smile that flashed across her lips every time she was winning sent heat flashing through his body.

And that wasn't the only problem.

Isabella reached past him for the dice, her warm skin pressing against his arm as she moved. The dark curls of her hair hung over her face, and he could smell roses when he breathed in.

He tensed, waiting for her to retreat again—but when she did, the softness of her breasts brushed against his shoulder, forcing him to swallow hard.

This was unbearable.

Because M knew what it was doing. The agency, or Madison Morgan herself, had picked his perfect woman—at least in one way. Isabella was beautiful, curvaceous, oozing an unconscious sex appeal that was driving him insane.

He had a whole week alone with the most beautiful woman he'd ever seen in real life, and he was going to spend it playing Monopoly.

This was why he needed to get out of the villa and *do* something. Sitting around only let him think and feel and imagine, and that wasn't good for either of them right now.

As soon as she'd passed go and collected her money, Matteo grabbed for the dice and rolled them. Isabella moved his piece for him, since it was on her side of the board, and gleefully shouted, 'Rent!'

Thank God. Handing over the remains of his pretend savings, he sprang to his feet. 'Then that's me out. You win. Uh… I need to go for a run.'

Her forehead creased adorably. *Not adorably. Just normally. Like any normal woman.*

'Didn't you already go for one this morning?'

Yes. Yes, he had. 'Gotta catch up on training, right?'

'Sure,' she replied, not sounding convinced. 'Um, I'll see you for dinner, then?'

'Definitely.'

Because even he wasn't as unchivalrous as to leave his only companion all alone for dinner. Nothing to do with the almost orgasmic look that crossed her face whenever she was eating the food here.

He was almost *certain* she wanted him too, not that she'd been obvious about it. It was the little things, the ones he only saw because he was looking for them. The way her eyes darkened when she smiled at him, the way she bit into her lower lip and looked away when he smiled back. The heat that seemed to sizzle between them, whenever they got too close...

In the end, he didn't bother changing into his running gear, and just walked straight out along the path that meandered down towards the edge of the lake and around it. He needed to think, not run, this time.

Identify the problem, Matteo. This was no different from a problem with a car, or a bend of the track he couldn't quite hit right. No different from any of the challenges in his life he'd overcome to get where he was now.

He'd taken trips and risks other people didn't even dream of. He'd trekked Machu Picchu, done solo skydives, skied mountains others just sat and looked at. He'd come from nothing and made his billions. He risked his money as easily as his life, and he *always* came out on top, whatever the concerns of his management team.

He beat the odds, every time.

And he wasn't going to be thrown off his game by a princess who was too scared to leave the house.

Maybe the problem wasn't that she was beautiful. He'd met many beautiful women in his life, and had plenty of them in his bed, come to that. But none of them had ever filled his mind the way Isabella had over the last day—to the point where even an innocent game of Monopoly had led to him imagining making love to her on top of the damned board.

Was it the princess thing? No. He'd never had any particular interest in royalty, and his money and his fame had put him in plenty of aristocratic company before now without problems. Royalty were just one more type of celebrity really, weren't they? And he had enough celebrity of his own.

Except…there was one aspect of the princess thing that made a difference.

The untouchable part.

Matteo groaned aloud as he realised, scaring a bird in a nearby tree into flapping off in a hurry. Lowering himself to sit on a flat rock by the water's edge, he looked out over the huge expanse of Lake Geneva towards the distant mountains and thought his way through to the heart of the problem.

He'd promised himself, even before he'd met her, that he'd keep this week light. That he'd focus on friendship. Because the woman he'd be spending the week with was looking for her perfect match, and he wasn't offering true love to *anyone*. He was there under false pretences, and it would be wrong to lead her on.

Except, of course, by making Isabella forbidden fruit, he only wanted her more. And the fact that she was a princess, that the royal family would never allow her to date him, let alone marry him, well...

Matteo had never done well with being told what he could and couldn't do. Even by himself.

So. He'd identified the problem. Now he just needed to figure out what to do about it. Because nothing had changed—

Wait.

Yes, it had.

He'd been assuming that Isabella was here looking for her Prince Charming. But she wasn't. She'd been manipulated into coming, just as he had.

She wasn't looking for love from him.

Matteo smiled to himself, as Lake Geneva shone in the June sunshine.

Because that opened up all sorts of possibilities.

* * *

Isabella was nowhere to be seen when he finally returned to the villa, so Matteo headed to his room and showered and changed for dinner. As he towelled off his hair, he heard movement on the balcony—but by the time he'd dressed and went to investigate, whoever had been out there had gone.

Their discreet housekeeping staff had left them another feast, though. Obviously they'd observed their preference for eating on the balcony and brought dinner straight to them this evening. Tonight's dinner, when he peeped under the silver cloche keeping it warm, appeared to be some sort of fish dish with rice that smelled amazing.

'Is it time for dinner?' Isabella appeared in her doorway. The jeans and T-shirt she'd worn during the day had been replaced by a bright red sundress, and the matching lipstick she wore made Matteo all the happier he'd figured out his issues during his walk.

She did appear subdued, though, and dinner passed relatively quietly, without any of the chatter they'd enjoyed at breakfast, or the night before.

Her eyes lit up as he unveiled the tiramisu waiting for them on the nearby trolley, though, and Matteo decided it was time the address the elephant in the room.

Except Isabella got there first.

'I think we need to talk,' she said as he reached for the serving spoon for the tiramisu.

'I agree,' he replied.

He heard her take a deep breath, as if steeling herself for something unpleasant. He added an extra spoonful of pudding into her bowl, just in case.

'The thing is…we're stuck here all week, right? Together. And since playing board games clearly isn't your cup of tea, neither of us are *actually* looking for true love, and we're both supposed to be staying out of trouble…what do you suggest we spend this week doing?' she asked.

Matteo handed her the over-full bowl of dessert and sat back in his chair, trying not to smile. She'd given him the perfect opening.

'Well, I see it as an opportunity.' He hadn't, until he'd spent the day trying to keep his hands off her. Now, it was all he could think of.

'An opportunity?' She took a spoonful of tiramisu and slipped it between her lips, her eyes fluttering shut with pleasure as she tasted it. 'Mmm, you have got to try this.'

It wasn't the pudding he wanted to try, though. It was her. He wanted to taste her lips, and the cream still lingering there. He wanted to kiss every inch of her curves. He wanted to learn all the other things he could do to coax that satisfied, pleasured moan from her mouth.

And after a day of fighting it, he was done.

'I will,' he said, swallowing. 'And yes, an opportunity. After all, we still have everything M promised, right? A week of seclusion. The freedom to do whatever we want, without anyone watching. And we were chosen to spend the time together because we're supposed to be perfectly matched. Compatible, if you like.'

What was the point of trying to resist a temptation that had been so perfectly selected to tempt him? If she didn't expect true love from him…what was stopping them?

Her eyes were open now, wide and wondering—so wide he could almost read the thoughts passing behind them. Maybe she hadn't been thinking them before, but now he could tell that her thoughts echoed his own. She was seeing the possibilities, too.

Matteo couldn't be the only one feeling the chemistry between them. That kind of sensation only happened when it went both ways, in his experience. And M had got one thing right, at least—the chemistry between them was like nothing he'd ever felt before.

He wanted to know where that would lead.

Where it could take them. And from the look in Isabella's eyes, she did too.

She wasn't saying anything, though. And he didn't want to rush her.

She was thinking about it. That was enough for tonight.

Leaning closer, over the table, Matteo dropped his voice to a low purr—the one an ex-girlfriend had told him sounded like his engine warming up. 'I'm not a prince, Isabella. And I've got no interest in being one, either. After this week, we'll both go our own ways, right? Back to the lives we live in our own worlds. But until then…why not make the most of the freedom we've been given this week? Live a little dangerously.'

Reaching out, he swept way the morsel of cream that clung to her full lips, then sucked his finger into his own mouth to taste it, hearing her breath hitch at his movements.

'I… I don't know.' He could feel her holding herself back. Was that just her royal upbringing, or something else? Was it just because he wasn't a prince? Because the attraction between them definitely wasn't all in his imagination. He could see it in her glassy eyes, pupils blown. In the way she swallowed and her tongue darted out to wet her bottom lip and, *God*, he wanted to kiss her.

But he wouldn't. Not until she told him herself that she wanted that too.

'Think about it,' he murmured. 'And I'll see you in the morning.'

Then he turned and headed for his lonely bedroom, knowing he wasn't going to be thinking about anything but her tonight.

CHAPTER FOUR

ISABELLA DID NOT have a second restful night.

She left the dinner dishes on the balcony and retreated to the calm, cool bedroom to follow her usual bedtime routine, just as she had the night before. A bath, with the lavender oil she always travelled with, followed by her skincare regime—the one her mother said would keep her looking 'acceptable' for longer. Then, wrapped up in her pale pink silk pyjamas, she curled up on the bed with her book.

She barely read a page.

In fact, she'd gone through her whole routine on autopilot.

Think about it, Matteo had said. It seemed as though she'd be doing nothing but.

He'd barely touched her—just removed a blob of cream from her lips. A mother or nanny might have done the same, brusquely or absently. But when *he* did it…

His fingertip brushing against her lip had

sent sparks firing through her body—sparks she hadn't been sure she was capable of even feeling, any more. That slight pressure had been enough for her to imagine his touch everywhere else—over every inch of her body.

There was no ambiguity in what he'd been suggesting. In fact, she was almost surprised neither of them had mentioned it before. Gianna had hinted at it, of course, but Isabella…

Isabella had suggested they play board games.

She groaned at the memory. How out of touch was she with men and romance that this idea hadn't occurred to her?

Except that was a lie, and Isabella tried hard not to lie—even to herself.

She *had* thought about it, from the moment she'd seen Matteo standing above her on the balcony and known he was supposed to be her perfect match. She'd thought about it every time he stood close enough for her to feel the heat of his skin or smell his cologne. Every time she'd brushed past him to retrieve the dice when they were playing. Every time he'd smiled at her or watched her enjoy dessert. She'd just been too scared of what that meant to even consider doing anything about the thought.

Now, snuggled down on the cool, crisp sheets,

Isabella stopped trying to ignore the possibility, and let herself think about it properly.

One week. No rules, no prying eyes, no consequences.

For this one week she could cut loose. And if she wanted, she could take Matteo as a lover—bring him to her bed and let him worship her body, and explore his in return. He'd made it clear that was how he'd choose to spend this week, rather than playing Monopoly.

She supposed that was a fairly common thing for him. She was sure his daredevil attitude to life continued into his romantic entanglements, too. She hadn't followed his career particularly closely, but even she'd seen enough clips on the Internet or in papers to know that he never dated the same woman twice, but always had a beauty on his arm whenever he wanted one. Picking up a woman for a week of debauchery and seduction was probably par for the course in his downtime.

But for her…

She hadn't been with a man since Nate, and even that had been a lie. She wasn't a virgin, but she definitely wasn't experienced, either. And honestly, since Nate she hadn't really been interested in anyone all. She knew there were plenty of stories on Augustian social media about her love life, but they were all fabrications.

Her heart had been broken, and her faith in people severely dented, by her first foray into love. It was one of the reasons she'd been so unsure about the whole idea of her 'perfect match' in the first place.

Except that wasn't what she was here for, and it wasn't what Matteo was offering, either.

He was offering a week of giving in to the chemistry between them. A week of pleasure, she was sure. A week of fun, strings-free.

And she wanted it. She had to admit that much to herself.

But was she brave enough to take it? Even knowing what had happened last time she'd let go in such a way?

She wasn't sure. And by the time she fell asleep that night she still hadn't decided.

Her dreams were filled with unfamiliar images—and feelings. The water of Lake Geneva, lapping around her. The scent of the flowers that grew in the pots on the balcony, mingled with the more familiar lavender of her pillows, and a spicy, new scent that she knew was Matteo himself.

Skin on skin, slick with water and want. That was all she remembered when she awoke, unsatisfied and frustrated, from a night of dreams.

And now she had to face him again.

Great.

Isabella took her time washing and dressing, trying to scrub the dreams from her body in case Matteo could see them on her, somehow. Or smell them, perhaps, the way she dreamt she could still smell him in the air around her.

But eventually she had to admit to herself that she was just postponing the inevitable. She had the whole rest of the week here in this glorious villa, beside this beautiful lake, with Matteo. Not making the most of it would be a terrible waste.

Throwing open the doors to the shared balcony that joined their bedrooms, Isabella let the morning air rush in, and felt her own breath rush out.

Once again, Matteo was already sitting at the table on the balcony. There were shadows under his eyes that suggested his sleep might have been as disturbed as her own. But he looked up as she appeared, and a slow smile spread across his face at the sight of her, making him look instantly younger. More free.

Was he remembering that moment last night, too? The one when he'd been close enough for her to kiss, if she'd moved her head just ever so slightly? Was he thinking about the suggestion he'd made to her?

The smirk on his face suggested he probably was.

'Good morning,' he said, his voice low and warm. 'Sleep well?'

She took her seat. 'Like a baby.' It wasn't a lie. Babies were notoriously bad sleepers, weren't they?

'Me too.' The smirk hadn't gone anywhere. 'So, how are we going to spend our second day in secluded paradise? Chess? Poker?'

He was teasing her now, but she didn't rise to it. Instead, she looked out over the lake, the balcony suddenly claustrophobic, despite all the fresh air. This villa was huge, and she knew that if she asked for space Matteo would give it to her. He wasn't the kind of man to press where he wasn't wanted, she could tell that already from the way he'd backed off last night after the merest suggestion of more.

The problem was, she wasn't at all sure she wanted him to keep backing off. But she wasn't certain enough to let him in, either.

She wanted him; she wasn't lying to herself about that any more. But it was *so* against The Rules. And beyond anything she'd let herself want for so long—ever since Nate. The desire she felt for Matteo...it was overwhelming, and terrifying.

And it felt amazing, all the same.

She stared out over the water and the mountains in the distance. The June air was warm and welcoming, but the breeze from the water kept things fresh in the shady trees that surrounded the villa.

She didn't want to be trapped inside today—otherwise, this villa was no better than the palace in Augusta that she'd escaped from.

Maybe she wasn't ready to take the risk of letting Matteo in quite yet. But perhaps she could take the tiny risk of letting herself out. Just a little bit.

One small first step towards where she was almost ready to admit she really wanted to go.

To bed, with Matteo.

Isabella placed her empty coffee cup down on her saucer. 'I'm going for a walk, down by the lake,' she said, before she could change her mind. That would give her time and space to keep figuring out what she wanted from this week. Time away from the allure of Matteo's smile, or those green eyes that pulled her in whenever she caught them.

Matteo grinned. 'Great! I'll come with you.'

There was a narrow path, leading away from the villa in the opposite direction from the easier one he'd taken for yesterday's walk, down the slope of the ground to the water's edge. Matteo hopped down it easily, hands in his pockets, then looked back to find Isabella picking her way along the uneven ground more cautiously.

'Need a hand?' He stretched out his arm to offer his assistance, but Isabella shook her head.

'I'm fine.'

That was a lie if ever he'd heard one. Oh, not with the path—he was sure she was more than capable of making her way down that alone.

But Princess Isabella of Augusta was not fine.

Perhaps it was just being away from the palace and out on her own for what, he imagined, had to be the first time in a long time. But he suspected it had more to do with the ideas he'd put in her head over dinner the night before.

She was a princess, not a casual hook-up in his usual fashion, he knew that. But still…they needed to find a way to entertain themselves this week, right? And since his usual methods of adrenaline-seeking were off the table, Matteo could only think of one good one.

Not to mention the fact that the more time he spent with her, the more inevitable them falling into bed together seemed. So why put it off? Why not enjoy the hell out of it while they had the time? Now he'd made the decision, Matteo was done denying what he wanted.

But back to the Princess.

After he'd retreated to his room the night before, Matteo had done a little internet research. Only natural, really, he figured. After all, she knew who *he* was, and was presumably familiar with his reputation. It was only fair that he use the tools at his disposal to put them on an equal footing. Thank goodness for high class Wi-Fi in such a remote spot.

Augusta, he'd learned, was a tiny little country—one of those ones squeezed between the bigger, more familiar European powers. Still, its monarchy had its fans—especially the next generation. Matteo was secure enough in his own masculinity to admit that Isabella's older brother, Leo, the Crown Prince, was handsome, built, and probably the subject of teenage Augustian girl fantasies, despite the fact he'd got married a few years before. Her sister, too, was married off, as were all the cousins and second cousins—at least, the ones over twenty-one.

Isabella, at twenty-eight, was already gaining articles about her being 'on the shelf', which seemed kind of ridiculous to Matteo, who was already five years older than that and had no intention of marrying any time soon. But it was different for royals, he supposed.

There'd been a short mention of a boyfriend in one of the articles from a few years ago, but nothing much more. And he'd avoided most of

the gossipy pieces; he knew from his own experience how inaccurate they could be.

'Okay?' he asked as Isabella reached the bottom of the path.

'Fine,' she said again.

He wished she'd stop saying that.

Because the thing was, Matteo had only
known the Princess for less than forty-eight
hours, and he already knew it was a lie. She was
beautiful, witty, bright and fun to be around—
and he thought that was more to do with her
natural personality than her royal training. She
didn't ask the 'have you travelled far?' or 'what
do you do?' questions he'd been asked on being
presented to other members of other royal families. She didn't keep up that screen of polite re-
serve, of smiling because she was supposed to
smile, or listening because she was supposed to
listen, not because she was happy or interested.

And yet…she was definitely holding back.
He could sense it in the straightness of her
back, the way she paused too long before an-
swering his questions. The way uncertainty
would flash behind her eyes whenever he got
too close.

He'd seen that before—in other women, and
in friends, too.

Someone had hurt her. Someone she loved.

Not that it was any of his business, he knew.

And yet…part of him wanted it to be.

She's just one more challenge, that's all, he told himself. And she wasn't even on Giovanni's list. He needed to let it go.

'Which way do you want to go?' he asked as they reached the edge of the water. The path, a little more established here, stretched out in both directions, surrounding this corner of Lake Geneva. To the right, it joined up with the path he thought he'd taken yesterday.

Matteo's geography was a little rusty, but he seemed to remember that the lake was *huge*, almost like an ocean between the countries of Switzerland and France. Driving in from the private airfield where he'd landed, he'd passed dozens of small lakeside towns and resorts, before disappearing into the trees that surrounded the villa he and Isabella were staying in.

Maybe he'd persuade Isabella to go explore some of them with him one day, once she trusted him a little more.

'That way.' She pointed to the left, seemingly randomly, but as they broke out of the tree cover Matteo decided it was a good choice, all the same. Up ahead was a small jetty, seemingly attached to their villa, since there were no other residences in sight. A speedboat, painted in white and blue, was moored up beside it practically calling his name; he would have to take that out on the water this week. Maybe he could even convince Isabella to join him in that adventure, if she wouldn't risk the towns...

There was also, he realised somewhat belatedly, another, much easier path down from this side of the villa. Oh, well; coming down the forest path had been an adventure. And wasn't that what he was known for?

'It's beautiful here, isn't it?' Isabella said.

He looked at her. The June sun beat down on her dark curls, making them shine so brightly they were almost white where the light hit. Her face was tilted up towards the sky, soaking in the warmth, her arms loose at her sides and her white cotton sundress dancing around her calves in the slight breeze.

She was beautiful. Never mind the damn lake.

Again, he felt that tug of lust down low in his belly, the one he'd been vaguely conscious of since the moment he first saw her, standing with her back to him on the terrace. 'It's gorgeous,' he replied, a beat too late.

Isabella turned to him and smiled. 'I'll race you to the jetty.'

And before he could even process her words, she was already running, racing towards the slatted wooden platform that jutted out over the water.

He could have caught her easily, if he'd started moving immediately. But instead he took a moment to watch her run, her hair flowing in the wind, her curved calves flashing under her thin white skirt.

Then he caught her.

In a few long strides, he reached her side and, as they approached the jetty, wrapped an arm around her waist to catch her, pulling her body tight against his as she laughed and he grinned against the warmth of her hair.

It was a game, a moment of lightness and fun…and then it changed.

Like a cloud passing over the sun, Matteo felt all the playfulness of the moment disappear in a shadow of an instant.

Her curves pressed against the planes of his body, soft and yielding in his arms, and for a second he almost forgot there was clothing between them at all. Her hair smelled of roses and sunshine, and it overwhelmed his senses. He heard her breath hitch in her throat and realised that he'd stopped breathing altogether.

He'd known she was beautiful. But like this, pressed against him as if the only place she belonged was in his arms…she was so much more.

She was magnificent.

He should let go. That would be the gentle-
manly thing to do. But how could he when this
felt so right?

'Matteo…' She twisted her head to look up
at him, her tongue darting out to moisten her
full lower lip in a way that made him groan
with want. He was so instantly, painfully hard,
pressed against her, she had to know exactly
how he felt. What he wanted. How he needed
her.

He'd expected to see uncertainty in her eyes.
But when he met her gaze with his own he
found only a reflection of his own want.

Lust surged through him as he hauled her
up until his mouth met hers. He kissed her the
way he'd wanted to since he first saw that lush
mouth of hers—deep and hard and as if there
were nothing more in the world but the two of
them.

And she kissed him back, matching his passion as she turned in his arms, raking her hands
up into his hair to hold him closer. God, how
had he thought this siren reserved and shy? Instead, she was everything he needed to remind
him he was still alive, still had adventures to
find, places to explore.

Like her entire naked body. Preferably now.
They'd been promised seclusion, right? He
hadn't seen another villa for miles before he

reached theirs. No one would see if he stripped her dress from her and made love to her here on the sun-warmed wood, right? And even if they did… Matteo was past caring.

But Isabella was not, it seemed.

As he reached for the straps holding her dress up and slowly pushed them down her arms, she wrenched her mouth away from his at last. Her eyes were still wild, her hair curling in all directions where he'd been running his hands through it. And her mouth—those gorgeous plump lips—was swollen from his kiss.

Matteo started to drop his hands from her body, but she grabbed them before he could, holding them between them, crushed against her breasts. His fingers itched to reach out and stroke the line of her neck, down past her collarbone and under the white cotton of her dress. But he made himself wait and listen.

This, he assumed, was where she told him all the reasons this was a bad idea, reminded him that she was a *princess*, so could never think of acting on the obvious attraction between them. He tried to prepare himself for the inevitable, even though his body was clearly still far more optimistic than his mind.

And then the Princess said, 'Race you to a bed.'

CHAPTER FIVE

ISABELLA DROPPED HIS HANDS, turned and started to run.

She had no real hope of being able to outrun Matteo—not that she really wanted to, for long. But if she acted fast enough, perhaps she could outrun the voice in her head reminding her of all the reasons that this was a terrible idea.

She didn't care. Not right now. And maybe that would come back to bite her later, but she'd deal with that then.

This was her week of freedom. Her week to be Isabella, not the Princess. Her week to find her own happiness, her own pleasure.

And from just one kiss, she already knew that Matteo Rossi could give her a hell of a lot more pleasure than anyone else in her life ever had.

Her blood pounded in her ears as she raced up the path towards the house—the simple, straight one, not the one through the trees they'd come down. She wasn't wasting any time getting back to the villa now she'd made her decision.

No, she hadn't decided. More…followed her instincts, for once.

From the moment Matteo had caught her, the instant she'd felt his body against hers, she'd known she was done fighting the attraction between them. Because if she left this villa at the end of the week without sampling everything he was offering, she knew that she'd regret it for the rest of her life.

She could hear Matteo's thudding footsteps on the path behind her, slow and steady, as she approached the villa. He was pacing himself, of course. He didn't want to beat her, and he wanted to save his energy for what would happen when he *did* catch her.

Isabella allowed herself a small, secret smile at the thought. God, she couldn't wait for him to catch her.

She risked a glance back over her shoulder and found him almost right behind her. Her heart was racing—was it because of the running, or the pursuit? Or because it knew what was coming next…

Finally, finally she reached her destination. Grabbing the handle of the large, sliding glass door that opened up the whole ground floor to the outside world, she yanked it open and tripped inside. Matteo's arm was around her waist in an instant, keeping her upright, keeping her close.

'Caught you,' he murmured into her ear, and she shivered in delight.

'I don't see a bed yet,' she whispered.

In response, Matteo swept her up into his arms and strode purposefully towards the stairs. 'We can fix that.'

Isabella laughed. 'You don't need to carry me!'

'I'm not risking you running away again.'

But she wouldn't, she knew. Maybe she *had* made a decision, after all.

One to make the most of every moment of freedom she had this week. One to put aside her fears and The Rules and her trust issues and go with her feelings instead. Her body, even.

Gianna had given her this week, and now Isabella was giving herself *this*.

She wasn't going to let herself back away again. Not for anything.

They'd barely made it up the first step, though, when a sharp, ringing sound rang out through the villa.

Matteo froze, mid step.

'Alarm?' Isabella asked.

'Phone,' Matteo corrected her.

The noise repeated. And repeated.

'Right. Of course.' She knew what a phone sounded like. It was just that in her world, a noise like that was more likely to be a fox setting off one of the proximity alarms at the palace, or a sightseer getting a little too enthusiastic about their visit and pushing through an alarmed barrier to a room that was out of bounds. 'Leave it.' It was the reckless kind of thing she did this week—ignoring phone calls and alarms.

The phone was still ringing. And Matteo was still holding her, motionless on the stairs, obviously at war within himself.

Finally, he sighed and put her down. 'It could be the security team,' he said, far too reasonably for her liking. 'If we don't answer, someone will come up here and interrupt us anyway. And I'd rather take the call fully clothed than deal with a burly security guard bursting in when I'm buried deep inside you.'

His voice dropped on the last part of his sentence, and Isabella felt it resonate through her body until she was throbbing with the need to feel him there, not just talking about it.

But instead, Matteo swept across the room, picked up the receiver and barked, 'Yes?'

As she watched, his demeanour softened a little even as his shoulders slumped in resignation. 'Madison. Hi. Yes, we both made it here okay.' He looked up and caught Isabella's gaze with his own, apology in his eyes. Then he chuckled at something the dating-agency owner had said, and he looked away. 'Getting you to check up on me, are they? Sure, sure, you always check in on day two. Well, you can tell my management team that I am staying out of trouble. The Princess and I have been for a lovely walk through the woods this morning, and around the lake to the jetty.'

Isabella smiled. The truth, if not the whole truth.

She could see the strain on Matteo's face as he tried to remain polite, to convince Madison—and presumably, by association, his team—that he was behaving. Not that she imagined they'd be complaining too much about his seducing her—or the other way around, if she was honest. After all, why send him on a dream date if they didn't want him to, well, find a little relaxation that way?

Still, this conversation was going on far too long for her liking. Isabella smiled. She had just the way to fix that.

If he'd honestly believed that this was just a courtesy call from Madison Morgan to check that they'd settled in okay, Matteo would have hung up in an instant. But he knew his team, his management. He knew Gabe.

He'd been ignoring his phone ever since Isabella had arrived, and that would have Gabe worried. So he'd found another way to check up on him. His manager had always been a little overprotective of the talent.

No, that wasn't fair. Gabe had always been overprotective of *him*. And if he'd set Madison up to make this call and Matteo didn't answer… well, those security guards would be bursting in again any moment. And he *really* didn't like being interrupted.

'Everything has been perfect,' he reassured Madison. *Everything apart from the timing of this phone call.* Because now Isabella had an excuse to overthink, to start listing all the reasons this was a bad idea. And that would lead to her changing her mind.

He could almost see the thoughts passing over her face as the occurred to her. She took a step back up the stairs, getting ready to run.

The attraction between them was undeniable, but even he had to admit the logistics weren't great. If he'd *actually* been looking for his one true love, he'd have been pretty pissed off. But as it was, this worked perfectly for him. Although he knew his team had been hoping this week might lead to a stable girlfriend for him, one who might take over responsibility for keeping his feet on the ground and the whole of him out of hospital for a while, that wasn't what Matteo wanted.

He just wanted Isabella, naked, under him, on top of him, and anywhere else she wanted, for the rest of this week. And Madison Morgan, matchmaker extraordinaire, was going to ruin that for him. The irony was actually painful.

But then, something changed, somewhere inside Isabella's mind. He'd probably never know exactly what, but he didn't really care.

A wicked smile flickered across her lips. And then, her eyes wide, she reached up and untied one of the bows at her shoulders that held up her dress.

Half of the white fabric of the bodice fell, sliding over the curve of her breast to hang under it, revealing the intricate, gossamer-thin lace of her strapless bra.

Matteo swallowed, his whole body tense with need. God, he wanted to drop the phone, race over there and take that perfect peak in his mouth.

But he also wanted to see what Isabella did next.

He didn't have long to wait. Slowly, deliberately, she reached up and untied the other bow.

The white sundress slipped away from her

skin, hanging around her hips, leaving her torso covered only by that see-through bra.

On the other end of the line, Madison was saying something about the boat at the jetty, but he wasn't listening. He was picturing his hands, his mouth, his body on those perfect curves. His gaze followed the gorgeous, undulating line of her, curving down over her shoulder, swelling over her breasts, dipping in for that narrow waist before flaring out again at her hips, where that damned sundress still hung, caught on the sheer generosity of her body.

'Right,' he said to Madison, with no idea what he was agreeing with.

Isabella smirked, as if she knew exactly how distracted he was. Maybe she did. Her eyes were almost black, and even at this distance he could tell she was breathing harder than her actions warranted.

She's turned on by this too. Thank God.

How had he thought, even for a moment, that this princess was buttoned up and boring?

'Yeah, of course,' he said, even though the words were meaningless. Matteo didn't take his eyes from Isabella for a moment.

And as he watched, she put her hands to her hips, and pushed the white cotton over them.

The dress fell to the floor, and Matteo gripped onto the edge of the telephone table hard, just in case he suddenly passed out from wanting her. It didn't seem completely impossible right now.

Had he ever been this hard, this desperate for a woman before? He didn't think so.

And he'd barely even touched her, kissed her.

God, he wanted to do so much more.

He let his gaze roam from her perfectly painted toes—her sandals abandoned by the door, he supposed—all the way up those long, shapely calves and thighs. He skirted past her wispy lace panties—because he knew there was no way he could keep control of himself if he lingered too long there—and continued along the curve of her waist, over her breasts, up to her face and met her gaze with his own.

The desire he saw there echoed the one throbbing through his body, and he knew he couldn't wait any longer. However exquisite the feeling of drawing out this pleasure had been, now he needed to act, not watch.

Isabella reached behind her back, unfastened her bra, and let it fall to the ground. Her magnificent breasts bobbed in front of him, and Matteo swore he was starting to see stars.

'Madison, I have to go.' He dropped the phone back onto its receiver and raced towards the stairs.

Definitely time to act.

* * *

Isabella laughed as she darted up the stairs before he could reach her, heading straight for her bedroom. A striptease for a man she barely knew hadn't exactly been on her to-do list for the week, but she *had* decided to go with her instincts for once...

And seeing the lust in Matteo's gaze as he'd watched her, she was glad she had. She'd felt powerful, in control of her own future for once—at least, her immediate future. The one that ended with her and Matteo in her bed. Taking control in such a way had calmed her re-emerging nerves about that part, too.

She careened around the corner into her bedroom, squealing as he caught her at last, wrapping an arm around her waist and hauling her to him, just as he'd done down by the lake.

'That was cruel,' he rasped against her ear, the desperation clear in his voice.

'I think the word you're looking for is "inspired",' she corrected him.

'That too.' He pressed a kiss to the patch of skin where her neck met her shoulders and she squirmed in his arms as pleasure fired through her nerves. 'You like that?'

'Mmm,' she agreed.

'Good.' Lifting her roughly, he dropped her down onto the bed from a just high enough height that she bounced. 'Let's find out what else you like.'

She'd thought that stripping for Matteo would be a treat for him. She hadn't anticipated how much it would turn her on, too.

She didn't do things like this—not least because, as a protected Princess of Augusta, she'd never had the chance.

Now she *had* that chance, just for the week. And she was going to take it.

Isabella moaned as Matteo kissed his way down her throat, over her collarbone, and further down, towards her breasts. With an appreciative noise from the back of his throat, he closed his mouth over her nipple, running his tongue around the sensitive nub until she writhed underneath him. God, that mouth wasn't only made for talking. She could feel him smiling against her skin before he released her with a pop, and moved across to give the other nipple the same treatment.

His hands weren't still either. As his mouth worked on her breasts, his hands brushed up and down her sides, caressing the curve of her hip. Then suddenly, they slipped underneath her, gripping her and pressing her against him.

Oh, she could feel him. He'd been keeping his weight off her, but now… She might be stripped down to her panties, but he was still fully clothed—and still, she could feel the hard length of him pressed against her bare skin, even through his jeans. Could imagine the size and the feel of him in her hand. In her mouth. Inside her…

It had been so, so long. And she'd spent too long thinking that the mistakes that came out of her last venture into lovemaking were her fault, that they meant she wasn't destined to have this in her life.

Yet here she was.

Matteo pressed one last kiss to her nipple then looked up, his green eyes bright as he met her gaze.

'You okay?' he asked.

'I will be.'

He smiled at that. 'Tell me what you need.'

You, inside me. The thought was instant, but saying the words was another matter. She bit her lip and watched his eyes darken.

'I need the words,' he said, sounding as though just talking was taking all of his self-control right now.

Maybe it was.

And yet, she knew if she said, *No, I can't, let's stop,* he would. Nate would have cajoled her, told her to stay with him a little longer and she'd change her mind.

Matteo would back off the second she said the words.

Maybe that was one of the reasons that, this time, she didn't want to.

'I want you to make love to me.' It came out a little faster, a little more desperate than she'd intended, but Matteo didn't seem to mind. Quite the opposite, in fact.

With a noise in the back of his throat that was almost a growl, he lowered his head and kissed her again, deeper and deeper. Which was wonderful, but wasn't getting him any more naked, so Isabella set about rectifying that instead, her fingers making quick work of the buttons of his shirt before she stripped it from his shoulders.

She let herself be distracted, for a moment, by all that lovely hard muscle and tanned skin, brushed with a dusting of dark hair. Closing her eyes, she ran her hands over the planes and dips of him, just as he'd done to her, memorising his body by touch alone.

But she couldn't allow herself to be *too* distracted. Opening her eyes again to find Matteo watching her, she held his gaze as she reached determinedly down to unfasten his jeans.

He helped her push his jeans and boxers down over those long, muscled legs, then stripped away her panties too, and suddenly there was nothing between them at all. Well, nothing that mattered right now.

She swallowed, as her gaze roamed down the length of him. It really had been a long time… but now she was here, she was almost dizzy with the need for him.

'Condom?' she asked breathily, as a reminder to herself that she hadn't completely lost her mind.

Matteo reached across to the small table beside the bed and pulled a strip of them from the drawer. Excellent.

'You're sure?' he asked again as he ripped open the packet.

'Very.' She took the condom from him and reached out to roll it securely in place. She wasn't taking any chances.

His breathing ragged, Matteo reached for her again, and Isabella went willingly into his arms, ready to embrace her freedom.

Making love to a princess, Matteo had decided, was probably the same as making love to any other woman.

But making love to Isabella? That was something new. Something special. Something totally unexpected—and a little unsettling. He'd thought this would be something else to tick off his list of adventures, another risk to take, even.

So why did it feel like something else?

The way she'd affected him since the moment he saw her should have been his first clue. He'd never wanted a woman the way he'd wanted Isabella. Wanted to touch her, to feel her in his arms, to smell her hair and taste her skin, to get as close to her as it was possible for two people to be.

And now that he was…he couldn't remember why he'd ever wanted to be anywhere else.

Holding himself up on his elbows, he let her guide him inside her, taking things at her pace, not his. Slowly, slowly he filled her, giving her time to adjust to him before he moved any more, watching her face carefully for every reaction.

Isabella's eyes were closed, her face clear and smooth, and for a brief, horrible moment it occurred to Matteo that she might not have done this before. That, as a princess, she might have been kept pure and chaste and…oh, God, what if he was her first?

Then her eyes flashed open and she gave him that wicked grin he'd seem when she was beating him at Monopoly. 'What are you waiting for, superstar? *Move.*'

And he did.

What had started slow and sweet and careful soon became more frantic, more desperate as they moved together, in perfect synchronicity. Isabella's hands clutched at his back, pulling her to him, driving him deeper with every thrust. Matteo had a feeling this would be over in an embarrassingly short space of time…but at least they had the rest of the week to make up for it.

Tugging her round, he flipped them so he was on his back, letting her ride him to her own pleasure. Long, loose dark curls hung down over her breasts as she moved, more languidly than he'd be capable of right now. Her chin tilted up, that aristocratic neck long and elegant, she bit down on her plump lower lip and Matteo thought he might be done for. Reaching up, he brushed the hair away from her breasts to cup them with his hands, and ran his fingers across her nipples, making her shiver above him.

Good. He needed to know this was affecting her the same way it was him.

'Isabella.' Her name came out as more of a moan than he'd intended, but it worked. Her eyes fluttered open and she looked down at him, her hips not losing their sanity-depriving rhythm for a moment.

The lust he saw in her eyes was the same one he felt coursing through his blood. And that was all it took for his baser instincts to take over.

Grabbing tight hold of her hips, he thrust up into her, gratified when she upped the speed of her own movements to match him. Not losing pace for a moment, he shifted one hand towards her core, teasing her with his fingers and driving her further and further to where he needed her to go.

And just when he thought he might lose his mind, she gasped and tightened around him, again and again as she cried out, her hips stuttering to a stop as he thrust once, twice, three times more…and felt his world explode.

'Oh, God.' Isabella slumped against his chest, sweaty and sated and salty sweet under his kisses. 'That was a good idea.'

'Glad you agree,' Matteo murmured against her skin. Although, 'good idea' weren't exactly the words he'd have chosen.

Transcendental, perhaps. Life-changing. Magical.

He blinked, and forced the thoughts away. It was just sex, same as any other sex he'd had with many other women. Sure, he was more attracted to Isabella than any of the other women he'd met lately—maybe ever. But that was just chemistry. Physical lust didn't mean anything more than an incredible time between the sheets.

And he was just lucky he got to experience

that for a week, before going back to the real world.

Isabella rolled away from him, leaving his skin cooling in the breeze from the open window as she lay beside him on the huge bed. Last night, lying in his own bed next door, he'd felt frustrated, adrift and alone. Before that, he'd felt unsettled and aroused and distracted by being around her.

Now, he only felt sated, relaxed and as if there was nowhere in the world he'd rather be.

He blinked at the thought. When had he last felt that way?

Speeding around the racetrack, it was a familiar feeling—especially as he cornered the last turn before the flag. But outside a racing car? That feeling was a lot harder to find.

On the top of a mountain, perhaps, looking out at the blue sky and great depths below. The second when he jumped from a plane, in the moments before he opened his parachute. Or when he sprang away from that cliffside and dived towards the water—before he broke his leg, of course.

But those highs only ever lasted until he reached solid ground again. Until the race was over, the adrenaline gone.

Until now.

He'd travelled the world on one adventure

after another, taking bigger and better risks, beating the odds—chasing the adrenaline high that reminded him he was alive, when so many others weren't. He'd taken chances that terrified the people around him so much that they'd sent him here, a last-ditch attempt to keep him safe and out of trouble.

And here, in Isabella's bed, he'd found that same peace he hunted for, that same high.

He just had a feeling it also came with a whole different sort of trouble.

Shifting onto his side, he watched Isabella's chest rise and fall as her breath slowly returned to normal.

'What are you thinking?' The question was out of his mouth before he had a chance to think whether he really wanted to know the answer. Because the odds of Princess Isabella of Augusta feeling the same as him right now seemed slim.

They both knew what this week was about, and it wasn't about transcendental feelings of satisfaction with the world. It wasn't about him finding a way to get his adrenaline high that didn't involve breaking any bones or taking any risks. Although he knew his team wouldn't mind if that was the case…

This wasn't a permanent solution. This was one week, that was all. Princess Isabella wasn't about to turn to him and tell him he'd so rocked her world that she loved him and wanted to make him her prince.

Which was good, because he didn't want that either.

Still, he couldn't help but smile when she turned her face towards his and said, 'Do you think there's any more food downstairs? I'm starving.'

CHAPTER SIX

ISABELLA HADN'T BEEN lying when she told Matteo she was hungry. But as he laughed and pulled on his jeans to go and raid the kitchen for her, she had to admit she hadn't been telling the whole truth, either.

She'd been thinking about taking chances. And how good it felt to take a risk for a change.

How buttoned up had her life been? Oh, maybe it wouldn't have been obvious to the casual onlooker. To someone who only knew her through her publicity photos or the palace's social media channels, she must seem the ultimate carefree princess. Never having to worry about the things that consumed so many other people's lives—like having a roof over their heads or enough money for food or keeping their family healthy and well. She'd always had a home at the palace—not to mention the 'summer house', a mansion in the hills of Augusta where the court could decamp in the hot weather—and royal property she could use throughout the country. She'd never had to prepare her own food, although since she'd been an adult her rooms had their own kitchen where she *could* cook, if she chose. Meals—no, banquets—had been the norm in the palace. The best doctors in the land—in Europe, the world—had been at their beck and call when required.

Isabella wasn't playing poor little rich girl. She knew how lucky she was.

It had just taken until now to realise what freedom truly felt like.

'I'm starting to think the staff here might be psychic.' Matteo pushed the door open with his knee, grinning as he appeared with a heavily laden tray. 'That, or we were a lot louder than I'd thought.'

Isabella pulled herself up to rest against the padded headboard, the sheets falling away from her body and leaving her bare from the waist up. 'What did they leave us?'

Matteo didn't answer immediately, apparently too busy admiring the view as his gaze roamed over her torso. Isabella didn't reach for the sheet to cover herself.

Yesterday, I would have done.

Yesterday, she'd have been embarrassed at the idea of someone listening to her having sex, and providing snacks ready for afters. Yesterday, she'd have blushed at the blatant ogling Matteo was indulging in.

Today…today she felt like a different person. Had done since that moment by the lake when she made her decision to embrace the possibilities of this week.

And she wasn't done embracing yet.

'I'm getting hungrier, here,' she teased, and Matteo gave her a shameless grin before setting the tray down on the bed and perching beside it.

'We've got coffee, cookies, some sort of gooey cake…plenty of sugar to keep our energy levels up.'

'Good.' She smiled up at him—her best princess smile. 'I think you're going to need it.'

Later, quite a lot later, when the cake was demolished to crumbs, the dregs of the coffee were cold, and Isabella's muscles were relaxed to the point of melting into the mattress, Matteo turned on his side and propped his head up on one hand.

'What changed your mind?' he asked as he studied her.

Isabella tried not to shift uncomfortably under his gaze. After all, the man had touched, tasted and loved every inch of her body over the course of the last handful of hours. Maybe longer; the sun looked a lot lower in the sky than she'd have thought…

'Changed my mind about what?'

'About me.' He raised his eyebrows. 'I mean, last night I definitely got "this is not behaviour befitting a princess" vibes from you. But today…' He left it hanging, their mutual nakedness doing all the talking for him.

'Maybe I just decided that I deserved a week off from being a princess.'

'And is that something you do often?'

'Never.' Except that was a lie, and here, beside him in her bed, Isabella found that she didn't *want* to lie to Matteo. Not even to preserve her reputation, or the monarchy of Augusta's reputation, come to that. 'Once,' she amended.

Curiosity flared behind Matteo's green eyes. 'Tell me? I mean, if you want to. Since you're just being Isabella this week, not a princess.'

'And this is something normal people do? Talk about their romantic disasters?' She wouldn't know. Her family had told her to lock it away inside her, pretend it never happened. Deny everything if Nate ever tried again to make another story out of it—although she suspected that Leo had paid him enough to make it worth his while to pretend it hadn't happened, either, after the initial flurry of press.

'This is something that normal people do,' Matteo confirmed. 'Well, some of them, anyway.'

'Not you?'

'I don't have romantic disasters.'

'Just cliff-diving ones.'

'Just those,' Matteo confirmed, with a grin.

'Although…that's not what the gossip magazines say.' Isabella shifted closer, her hands under her head as she curled towards him. 'They're forever talking about which heart you've broken now.'

Matteo rolled his eyes. 'You shouldn't pay any attention to them. They'll say anything to get people to buy a copy.'

'I don't know,' Isabella teased. 'There are a lot of photos of you…'

He reached over to brush his hand over her waist, almost light enough to tickle, before pulling her closer. 'Is this the part where I tell you none of them meant anything before you?'

It was her turn to roll her eyes, now. 'If this was a normal M dating agency week of passion, or whatever they call it, probably. But I think we both know neither of us are here for *that*. So the truth will do just fine instead, thank you very much.'

Matteo loosened his hold on her side, and

flopped onto his back. 'The *truth*? No one ever seems to care about that.'

'I do.' Because she knew she couldn't trust herself to interpret the world without it. People lied, all the time, and she wasn't sophisticated enough in the way of life outside the palace to even tell when it was happening.

'Fine. I like women—I like their company, and, well, I like sex.'

'I noticed,' Isabella said, with a smirk.

She didn't add, 'So do I.' Because she hadn't known that she did, not like this. Not until today.

And that was a discovery she was still adjusting to.

'But I'm always upfront with women about what I can offer,' Matteo went on, oblivious to her omission. 'I'm not in the market for a serious relationship, or anything more than a few nights of fun. I've got too many other things to do.'

'Like go cliff diving.'

'And win world championships.'

Isabella stretched out her legs under the thin sheets, feeling her well-used muscles protest at still being expected to move. 'But you've done both of those things now,' she pointed out. 'What else is on your list?'

There was a pause she didn't expect after

her question. Not one that felt as though Matteo was trying to think of something to say, or remember what daring plans he had next. More as though he was trying to decide whether to share it with her.

She wondered how outrageous it had to be, for that.

Finally, he moved to sit up against the headboard, and reached for his phone, swiping across the screen a few times before handing it to her.

She'd expected a website or a booking email or something—perhaps for deep-sea diving in the Red Sea, or a trek into the Himalayas. Instead, she found herself looking at a photo of a handwritten list.

He had an actual list.

Except…she frowned at the carefully printed words at the top of the page in the photo.

Giovanni Rossi's Bucket List

This wasn't Matteo's list. Even though she could see that he'd carefully crossed out plenty of items on it—including cliff diving. And becoming the racing world champion.

'I don't understand,' she said, handing back the phone.

Matteo took it from her, glanced at the screen

with an indecipherable look on his face, then placed it back on the table beside him. He looked…lost, somehow. She hadn't expected that from him, especially after the self-assuredness he'd shown in bed.

On impulse, she nestled closer, until he wrapped one arm around her shoulder as she rested her head on his firm chest.

'My brother,' he said, eventually. 'Giovanni. He was three years older than me.'

Isabella heard the *was* and knew that nothing that followed was going to be good.

'He was the daredevil, when we were kids,' Matteo went on, a fond smile on his face. 'Always the one getting into scrapes or trying the impossible just to prove that he could.'

He fell silent, and Isabella could feel the weight of that silence in the air around them.

'What happened to him?' she asked, when she couldn't bear it any longer.

She'd braced herself for a car accident, or some other sort of dangerous, reckless end. Which was why Matteo's reply made her gasp at the tragedy of it all.

'He was diagnosed with terminal cancer when I was sixteen.' His words were flat, emotionless, but Isabella could tell that was through practice. He said it the same way she said Nate's name, these days, and it had taken her years to perfect that emptiness between the syllables. *Nath-an-ial. Ter-min-al.* They sounded the same in her head.

'I'm so sorry, Matteo.' Isabella pressed a soft kiss to his skin and wished there were more she could do. But grief was grief, wasn't it? Whatever the cause, it was personal, and permanent.

He shrugged, and she felt the shift of his muscles under her cheek. 'It was a lot of years ago, now. Seventeen, almost.'

'Still. He was your brother.' Nathanial had been her world, and he didn't even have the good grace to be *dead.*

'Yeah.' Matteo slumped a little lower against the headboard, pulling her closer until her whole body half covered his. 'After he got sick…he made this list. All the things he'd wanted to do in his life but was never going to get the chance. I… I helped him. Because I think, even then, I thought he was going to get better. I thought it would give him something to look forward to, once the treatment was over. But instead…' She felt him swallow and wrapped her arm a little tighter around him. 'He died. And I was just left with this list. So I promised myself— promised him, really—that I'd do every single damn thing on it. Everything he didn't have time to do. Everything that was taken from him. And I am. I have.'

Become world champion. The list item floated in front of her mind's eye. Had Matteo based his whole career on his brother's dying wish list?

She couldn't ask that. She'd only known the man a couple of days, however much some algorithm somewhere said she was his perfect match.

But she could hear the grief in his voice— still there, not diminished at all by every challenge he crossed off his brother's bucket list. Unresolved.

'So what's next?' she asked instead. 'What's left on the list?' Because as far as she could tell, almost everything had been crossed off.

'Well, even Giovanni didn't envision making love to a princess,' Matteo joked, although there wasn't any real humour in his voice. 'So… I guess I'm pretty much done. Becoming world champion…that was his big dream, and I did it. And went cliff diving to celebrate.'

Isabella half smiled at that. 'I guess that means you'll have to start writing your own list now, then, huh?'

'I guess it does.' There was a hint of amazement, disbelief even, in his tone. But it was gone before she could even be totally sure it was there at all, as he twisted them around so she was underneath him again, and all she could think about was how right his body felt against hers. As if they were two parts of the same whole.

'But the list can wait?' she guessed as he pressed her further into the mattress, his arousal obvious against her belly.

'The list can *definitely* wait,' he agreed, before kissing her.

She hadn't answered his question.

Matteo didn't realise it until he awoke to the early morning light filtering through the gauzy curtains that barely covered the glass front of the villa. In fairness, he'd been far more pre-occupied with all the things she *had* been telling him—*more, now, again*—to focus on the conversation she'd sidestepped.

But lying there in the pale June dawn, with Isabella's body curled against his, he realised, and he wondered.

How had she persuaded him to tell all his secrets about Giovanni, about the list, about why he did the things he did, and still managed to evade telling him *anything* about herself? In fact, beyond the small detail of her being a princess, he wasn't sure he'd found out anything personal about her at all.

Was that part of being royal? The ability to ask polite questions and listen to the answers without ever giving anything in return? He didn't know. Isabella was the first royal he'd ever spent real time with, beyond the polite niceties, and he had a suspicion that she wasn't exactly typical.

He looked down at her, sleeping in his arms, and considered what he *did* know about her.

She wasn't looking for true love.

She hadn't been enamoured of any of the suitable prospective husbands Augusta had thrown up.

She hadn't come here through her own choice.

She wanted a break from being a princess— and she'd done that only once before…

What had happened then? Matteo was willing to place money that someone had hurt her. Someone had made her this way—cautious and careful. And if she was letting that go this week, with him… Matteo wasn't sure he could bear to see her go back to her buttoned-up ways afterwards.

Ever since he'd admitted that the chemistry between them was unavoidable, he'd hoped. He'd flirted and he'd hinted and he'd hoped— but he hadn't really expected. He'd figured a week of frustration and an inappropriate royal crush was probably punishment from the universe for something—maybe the broken leg, maybe the hearts he knew he'd broken, even when he'd been trying not to.

But he hadn't imagined this. Hadn't dreamt for a moment that their second full day together would lead to a race to the jetty and that kiss… not to mention everything that came after.

His position hadn't changed; he was the same man who'd seen a curvaceous brunette on the terrace below and hoped.

But Isabella…she'd become someone new overnight. Consciously, intentionally. She'd made a decision to be Just Isabella, rather than the Princess—but Matteo knew without her having to say the words that it wasn't a permanent change. This week was a holiday from being herself. Except, having seen how free and alive she seemed… Didn't she deserve to be that way all the time?

He wondered if he could convince her. If he could show her, in the days they had left together, that she could be whoever she wanted to be—not just in Lake Geneva, but in Augusta, too.

To do that, he suspected he'd need to get her to open up and tell him the story of the last time she tossed aside her crown for a while. And perhaps that was something she needed to work up to.

So he'd start small instead. See if he could

show the Princess that taking risks could be fun, sometimes. Even *outside* the bedroom.

Isabella stirred in his arms, and Matteo smiled to himself as he bent to kiss the top of her head, settling more comfortably down beside her. He wouldn't sleep any more, he knew, not now he had adventures to plan. But she was going to need her rest.

She wanted a week off from being a princess? Well, then... Matteo was going to give her the best week's holiday she could imagine.

And maybe by the end of it, she wouldn't want to stop.

'So, what are we going to do today?' Isabella asked, some time later that morning, as they shared coffee and a late breakfast on the balcony outside their rooms.

Matteo raised his eyebrows in what he'd been told was an expressive manner, and she rolled her eyes.

'Is your plan to spend the *whole* week here in bed?' It wasn't, of course. But he couldn't quite tell if she was actually disapproving of that idea, or just felt some princessy need to pretend she was.

'Would that be such a terrible plan?'

When she smiled, her dimples popped into existence, and it made Matteo smile back, every time. They didn't show up, he'd noticed, in her official Princess Isabella smile, the one she'd given him that first night they'd met—the smile she was displaying in every single photo of her that seemed to be in the public domain, at least the ones that he'd been able to find online.

The dimples only appeared when she was truly smiling with happiness or amusement. Matteo had started counting the number of times he got to see them, and the total was already gratifyingly high.

'Maybe not *terrible*, exactly,' she said, her voice a soft purr. 'But I figure we might need a small break. Sometimes.'

Matteo sighed dramatically. 'Oh, I suppose you're right.'

She tossed a small piece of bread at him, then giggled and ducked when he tried to throw one back.

'Actually, I had thought we might go on a small adventure today,' he said, once the mini food fight had died down.

Across the table, Isabella stilled with what he knew instinctively was apprehension. Fear, even. Fear that felt more than just a general nervousness of the unknown, somehow.

'What sort of an adventure?' Her tone was cautious. Matteo supposed he didn't blame her.

After all, he *was* famous for choosing the more extreme sort of adventures.

'I'm not going to force you to go skydiving or anything,' he said to reassure her. She didn't look particularly reassured. 'I thought we might take the boat out on the lake.'

She blinked. 'Boat?'

'The one that was tied up by the jetty. We saw it yesterday?'

Her cheeks turned pink. 'Oh, yes. Of course.'

'You did *see* the boat, right, Isabella?' he teased. 'I mean, you weren't so distracted by something that you failed to even notice the big boat tied up right next to you?' Okay, so it was quite a small boat in reality, but the point still held. She'd been so focused on his kisses, his touch, she'd lost all track of her surroundings.

The thought made his body start to tighten, and he was reconsidering the whole boat-trip idea when she tossed another piece of bread at him—this time, covered in jam.

'I saw the boat,' she said shortly, and he was fairly sure it was a lie. 'But do you really think we should take it out? I mean, I don't know anything about boats. Would we need to take one of the security team with us?'

'It's a fairly basic boat; I've driven them before. And there are life jackets here somewhere, I'm sure. We'll be fine. We won't even go too far from the villa, if you don't want to.' It was the smallest step he could think of for her to take, after she'd already taken the much bigger one of allowing him into her bed.

But it could be the first step to a new mindset for her. One where she didn't always automatically say no to things, until she was compelled to change her mind by events—or, in their case, sheer physical chemistry.

She looked down at her hands, suddenly the reserved, unsure Princess she'd been on arrival again—rather than the mischievous Isabella who tossed bread at him and made him come completely undone in bed. He watched as she came to a decision, lifted her chin and, with a determination he didn't really feel the suggestion warranted, said, 'Okay, then. We'll go out on the lake.'

Matteo smiled to himself. Stage one of his plan was complete.

CHAPTER SEVEN

Isabella was not at all sure that this was a good idea.

On the face of it, a short trip out on a boat on a lake, still miles away from anywhere, wasn't exactly a dangerous threat. But she was compiling a mental list of reasons this could be a disaster anyway.

1) They could capsize and drown, despite their life jackets.
2) Some paparazzi on a boat might find them and take photos through those ridiculous long lenses they had, and then her parents would know she wasn't with Sofia and it would be like Nathanial all over again.
3)...

Okay, that was all she had for now. But surely they were reason enough not to risk it?

She sat, tucked up in her life jacket, at the far end of the small boat from where Matteo was starting the engine. Despite the life jacket he wore—at her insistence—she could still enjoy the sight of his arm muscles as he worked to untie them from the jetty, the thick muscles of his thighs as he braced himself against the movement of the boat. She swallowed as she watched a bead of sweat work its way down his neck in the bright June sunlight…

Right.

3) They might not be able to keep their hands off each other, even on a damn boat, and then they'd take their life jackets off and cause the boat to capsize and then they'd definitely drown. Probably while paparazzi took photos of her naked, and it would be even worse than everything with Nathanial had been.

'You're catastrophising,' Matteo said mildly as the boat chugged away from the jetty.

Isabella blinked. 'I'm what?'

'You're thinking about all the things that could possibly go wrong out here on the water.'

'No, I'm…' He gave her a look, and she sighed. 'Fine, I'm catastrophising. But that's what keeps me safe—thinking about all the things that could go wrong *before* they happen.'

It was a lesson her father and mother had drilled into her after Nate. That she was not somebody who could just take chances, or jump at opportunities and see where they led, or—and this one was said with a certain amount of disgusted disbelief—*follow her heart*.

She was a Princess of Augusta, and with that privilege came expectations, amongst them the always unstated rule that she would not cause any sort of scandal to fall upon the royal house.

Well, unstated until that horrible week after Nate had left, at which point it was stated quite firmly and repeatedly, as if she had somehow missed it in the undercurrents of her upbringing.

She hadn't, of course. She'd just believed that love trumped duty somehow. She'd believed in happy endings, and in everything working out for the best.

She knew better than that now.

She knew better than to be on this boat. To be in Lake Geneva at all. To be spending the week in the bed of a *most* unsuitable man.

But she was doing those things anyway, even though she knew what her parents, her brother would say.

You're making the same mistakes all over again.

Except Matteo wasn't Nate, and they weren't in Augusta, where her every move was tracked and recorded and reported. There was a privacy agreement in place with the M agency; she'd checked.

They were alone in this part of the lake; the sun was shining down and it was a beautiful day. She should relax and enjoy it.

Except she couldn't.

Matteo settled himself opposite her in the small boat, where he could watch her *and* where they were going, which she appreciated.

'Can you trust *me* to keep you safe?' he asked softly. 'Just for today?'

On the face of it, it was a ridiculous question. He was a risk-taking daredevil, known for his chequered history with women and famous for driving too fast around racetracks. He was the *last* person anyone should trust to keep them safe, right?

But once again, Isabella's heart spoke louder than her head. 'Yes,' she said gently. 'I trust you.'

Matteo smiled, as warm as the June sun. 'Good. Then sit back and enjoy the trip.'

The lake was surprisingly peaceful, once she'd stopped catastrophising. Isabella leaned back against the edge of the boat and tipped her chin so the sun streamed down on her face as the air brushed past her, raising the ends of her shorter curls around her shoulders.

'You are very distracting up there, you know,' Matteo said, and when she looked up, he was watching her intently.

'If you try and seduce me here we'll capsize the boat.' That wasn't catastrophising. That was physics. She knew how…vigorous their love-making could get.

'More's the pity.' Shutting off the small engine, he let the boat drift a little on the water. 'Well, if seduction is off the table, how about lunch?'

Isabella sat up with interest. 'We have lunch?'

'Of course, we have lunch.' Matteo grinned. 'I found it ready for us in the kitchen before we left, all packed up in a cool bag.'

'The invisible servants really do know their stuff.' Had they heard them talking about going out on the boat, or just guessed when Matteo went searching for life jackets? Either way, they were as good at anticipating their needs as any of the staff at the royal palace. Leo or her father would probably want to steal them if they knew about their existence.

Which they wouldn't. Because once this week was over, Isabella would never speak of it again, and she and Matteo would be the only people in the world who ever knew it happened.

She'd never speak to Matteo again either, probably. Certainly never make love to him again.

'Hey.' Matteo frowned as he paused in pulling out the food from the bag. 'What just happened? You look like the sun just disappeared.'

Isabella forced a smile, shaking her head to rid it of the thoughts. They wouldn't go. 'It's nothing,' she said, when it was clear that her smile wasn't enough to convince him. 'I was just thinking about what happens after this week is over.'

He stilled for a moment, then placed the container of strawberries he was holding on the seat between them that was serving as a table.

'You mean between us? Or for you?'

'Both, I suppose.'

'Well, I expect that depends on you, really, doesn't it?' he said, his tone careful.

He really was from a different world if he believed that. 'Not exactly.'

'Because of the princess thing?'

Her whole life reduced to a 'princess thing'.

'Because there are expectations placed on me.'

'Stay out of trouble and marry a duke? Isn't that about the size of it?' He made it sound like nothing. 'Because the thing is, Isabella, I kind of had the feeling that princesses were people too. Real flesh and blood people, who felt things and wanted things and deserved to live their lives the way they wanted.'

She could feel his words in her veins, filling her body with the hope of them. Reaching across the seat between them, he ran his fingers up her hand, before circling her wrist with them, the pads of his fingertips resting on her pulse point, feeling the beat of her heart as it thrummed through her.

'See?' he whispered. 'Not just a princess.'

Isabella pulled her hand away. 'Maybe not. But I *am* a Princess of Augusta, and that means something. Maybe not to you, but to my family, my country. And to me.'

How had this conversation got so deep, so fast? She wanted to go back to tossing jammy bread at him or sinking her body down on top of his.

They should have just stayed in bed today after all. This whole thing was much easier to navigate between the sheets than out of them.

He sat back, studying her so keenly that she had to force herself not to fidget under his gaze. 'Wouldn't your family just want you to be happy?'

She almost laughed, the idea was so absurd. 'Have you *met* many kings and queens?'

'A few,' he replied, with a shrug. 'But I'll admit

I never had time to discuss their daughters' sex lives with them.'

That did make her laugh, despite herself. How did he do that? Always lighten the moment, just when she was getting down?

'So what would the obedient Princess of Augusta do next?' he asked.

That one was easy. 'She'd go home to the palace and continue life as always. Public engagements, charity events, hospital visits, that sort of thing.' When she couldn't get out of them.

'And blind dates with aristocrats you already know you don't want to marry.'

'That, too.' But in some ways, Isabella had come to realise, that was better than the alternative. Because at least when she went into something knowing it wasn't for ever, that it wasn't even what she wanted, her heart couldn't be broken at the end of it. Not this time.

'Okay.' He leant forward, his forearms resting on those muscled thighs as he held her gaze. 'And what does *Isabella* want to happen next?'

Something else. She had no idea what, but there had to be more than just that, didn't there?

Except last time she'd tried to reach for it, her whole world had almost come crashing down.

'The same thing,' she said coldly. 'I *am* the Princess, after all.'

'Of course.' His eyes were sad. 'And I don't

suppose the Princess would be allowed to socialise with a reckless, common-born racing-car driver, either.'

'I don't suppose she would.' Isabella ignored the sharp, short pain in her chest at the thought.

Matteo turned away, his attention apparently back on steering the boat again, even though they weren't moving. 'Then it's just as well we agreed at the outset that this was just for the week. We can have all the fun we want together, then go back to our real lives as if it never happened.'

'Just as well,' she echoed, and wondered how to convince herself that she wasn't lying.

Their boat trip hadn't exactly given him the information he'd hoped for from Isabella, but Matteo had to admit it had crystallised exactly where they both stood in their current situations.

They'd agreed that first night that this could only be for the week, and it wasn't as if he was even looking to change that. But the idea of Isabella being stuck in a life that was so obviously suffocating her...that unsettled him. A lot.

Still, she was a princess. Maybe that royal status—and the money, prestige and luxury that went with it—was more important to her than happiness, or freedom. It would be for a lot of people, he knew. Money might not buy happiness, but it could buy a hell of a lot of other things, as he'd discovered as his career had progressed, and the prize pots and sponsorship deals got bigger.

Matteo wouldn't judge. Well, he wouldn't judge *much*.

But he might feel a little bit of pity.

They'd separated and gone to their own rooms after their outing on the lake, both intuiting the need for a break from the unrelenting closeness of the past day or two. But it was already Thursday, and Matteo knew that their time together was limited; he didn't want to waste any more of it. Four days down and three more to go...

He knew he should just relax and enjoy Isabella's company while he had it. But somehow, that wasn't enough. He needed...what, exactly? To help her? To change her?

Or just to know that he'd had an impact on her life. That this week had meant something to her.

Because he was starting to feel as if seven days with Princess Isabella of Augusta might have more of an impact on his life than he'd ever imagined it could.

At the end of it, he'd walk away with a smile and a kiss and a thank you, the way he did with all of his love affairs. And he was perfectly happy with that plan.

He just didn't try to fool himself any more that forgetting Isabella would be as easy as forgetting any of the women who had come before her.

M knew what it was doing, after all. The dating agency had found him someone who, in another world, could have been his perfect match. He'd thought that meant someone like him—someone to take adventures and risks with, because she had the same adventurer's spirit as him.

Instead, they'd given him someone who needed him. Someone who he could ease out of her comfort zone, even while she calmed him. Not to the point of being a different person—he was still hankering for his next adventure. But when he was with her…it was as if she soothed his restless edges. As if he could rest for a while, between risks.

Being needed reminded him of his brother. Being soothed reminded him of his mother. The two people he'd loved most in the world, both of them gone, now.

And Isabella…she could be…

No.

He didn't want that kind of love again—not when he knew how easily it could be taken from him, the way his brother and his mother had been. And he didn't want the obligations love forced on him, either. He'd seen it with other drivers on his team, and in races. They fell in love, they got married, started families even—and that was when they lost their edge. Because taking risks for themselves was easy; taking risks for people they loved was another game entirely. One that not many were made to play.

He needed those restless, reckless edges of his. He couldn't let Isabella smooth them down too much, whatever Gabe and the others hoped.

Even if he had wanted to follow up on this dream date matching, once the week was over, it wasn't what Isabella wanted either. She wanted to go back to a life he could never be a part of. Her stifling, royal life.

So really, there was no point thinking about what happened after this week until it was over. There'd be another adventure waiting for him and he'd take it, as he always did. Giovanni's list might be finished, but there were more adventures that his brother had never even dreamed of. Not to mention a racing career to get back to. He still had two lives to live, to make the most of, for Giovanni's sake.

All the same, when he heard movement out on the balcony that linked his bedroom to Isabella's, he couldn't help but head straight for the door.

Three days.

He couldn't afford to waste any of them.

'When do you think they put this out here?' Isabella didn't turn around as she asked the question, her back still towards him. Apparently she was as attuned to his movements as he was to hers.

He turned his gaze from the way her curls were swept over one bare shoulder, above a thin, strapless sundress that clung to her curves down over her hips, then flared out to swirl around her legs to mid-calf. On the table in the centre of the balcony was another feast, ready for their evening meal. How had the servants got that there without him noticing? Okay, he'd been preoccupied with his thoughts of Isabella, but still...

'The staff here are starting to get a little creepy now.' He took his seat, grinning up at her as she laughed.

'Well, as long as they keep the food coming.'

'True.' She sat down opposite him, the evening sunlight sinking into her midnight hair, the most beautiful woman he'd ever seen in real life—and the most unattainable.

Yeah, there was no way he was going to be forgetting Isabella of Augusta any time soon.

Which meant he had to make sure she didn't forget him, either.

They'd do this on the terms they'd agreed—one week, then it never happened. But while the rest of the world might never know about their week, he needed to be sure that *Isabella* would keep it with her. Maybe even let it loosen her up a bit.

It was the one thing he *could* give her. A parting gift, say.

They ate their meal in companionable silence, their only conversation comments on the food, or the wine. But under their sparse words, Matteo could feel all the things they weren't saying.

Would they really make it the whole week without any of them coming out? He doubted it.

'I was thinking about tomorrow,' he said as Isabella finished off her chocolate dessert.

He loved watching her eat, loved the secret smile as her mouth curved around her dessert spoon and she savoured the taste. He knew now that she looked the same way when she wrapped her mouth around him, and he knew also that he'd never forget that. The image of her sinking down to her knees in front of him, hands on his thighs as she eyed him up, was burnt into his memory for ever. Thankfully.

She swallowed her dessert, and he swallowed his thoughts.

'What about tomorrow?' she asked.

'How would you feel about another little adventure?'

Before you go back to locking yourself up in that palace again.

She froze, just for a moment, her eyes darting to one side as she formed her response. 'An adventure? What sort of an adventure?'

He was pushing her, faster than she wanted to go. But they had so little time left…

'I thought we could slip away from here, take my car out to the nearest town, have a look around?' How could they come all the way to Lake Geneva and not see anything more than a villa and the water and the views? 'You know I'm not one for sitting around, doing nothing. And as you so rightly pointed out, we can't spend *all* week in bed. So we need to find some other things to do. Right?'

Isabella wasn't looking so sure, however.

'What about our security detail?' That wasn't a no. He'd take it.

He flashed her his most wicked grin. '*Cara*, I'm a racing-car driver. If you think I can't lose two guys in a big black car on these roads, you really haven't been paying attention.'

Isabella clamped her sun hat to her head with one hand and grabbed hold of the car seat beneath her with the other. Oh, how on earth had he got her to agree to this?

Actually, she admitted to herself, she knew *exactly* how. He'd fed her the remains of his chocolate pudding, then moved the table aside to kiss her—first her mouth, then her neck, then down to her breasts, pulling the elasticated top of her strapless dress to her waist, effortlessly. Just as she'd imagined him doing when she'd put it on that evening.

And then he'd pulled the whole thing down her body, nudging her to lift her hips from the chair so he could drag the fabric down her legs, slow enough to drive her crazy as he followed it with his kisses…

Isabella blushed at the memory, but she had to admit it *had* been convincing. She'd agreed to today's day trip easily, breathlessly, by the time he was done. She'd let him make love to her out there on the balcony, in full view of anyone who cared to be looking—which she hoped was nobody, but you never really knew with those long lenses, did you? Plus there was the mysterious villa staff, and the security team—

The security team Matteo had effectively out-driven and lost ten minutes ago, with a driving manoeuvre she'd never seen anyone pull on an actual road before. She was fairly sure it would have got him disqualified on a racetrack, too.

'Where did you learn to drive like that?' she asked as they took another corner at speed. The road they were on now followed the line of Lake Geneva, past more villas and wooded areas. Hopefully the security team were still circling the lake in the opposite direction, unaware of Matteo's clever double-back.

'I took a police driving course,' Matteo said, driving with one hand on the wheel, the other on her thigh. 'Made friends with one of the instructors, and even got to go out with the *polizia* a couple of times.'

'Of course, you did.' Because there was excitement, risk there that he couldn't find in everyday life. That was what Matteo Rossi lived for, right?

And now she was living it with him—ditching her security team, heading out to some town she'd never heard of with a man she'd only known a few days... God, she'd been here before when she was young and stupid, and she'd sworn she'd never do anything like this again.

But then Matteo had stripped her naked on the balcony and made love to her on a blanket until she'd seen metaphorical stars as well as the ones in the sky above her. And suddenly she couldn't say no to him.

It really was a good thing that they only had a week together. Any longer and who knew what he'd talk her into? Selling the Crown Jewels of Augusta on eBay to finance a cave-diving trip, or something, probably.

One week of taking risks with Matteo. She had to admit, it wasn't what she'd expected from her early summer break.

Her phone buzzed in the pocket of her sundress, and she pulled it out, not surprised to see Gianna's number on the screen.

'Tell them you're fine and you'll be back later tonight,' Matteo said as she stared at the ringing phone. 'It's easy.'

Biting her lip, Isabella pressed answer.

'Your Highness? Oh, thank goodness. Is everything okay? The security team at the villa—'

'Everything is fine, Gianna,' she interrupted, keeping her voice as calm as possible, and hoping Gianna couldn't tell how far over the speed limit Matteo had been going. He'd slowed down a little now they were away from the villa, enough that she could just about hear Gianna over the rushing air racing over the convertible. 'You can tell the security team not to worry. We'll be back tonight.'

'Are you sure?' Despite the wind, Isabella could still hear the worry in her friend's voice.

She looked over at Matteo behind the wheel, sunglasses in place, smiling as he drove through the Swiss countryside.

'Yes,' she said. 'I'm sure.'

Because it might only be for a week, but she wasn't ready to start saying 'no' to Matteo Rossi just yet.

Isabella lost track of how long they'd been driving, focused instead on Matteo's hand on her thigh, and the secret smile on his face under his sunglasses. Was this how normal women felt? Out for a drive with their…no, she wasn't sure there *was* a word for what she and Matteo were. Lovers, she supposed, was closest. But somehow it didn't feel right. It wasn't…enough, somehow. Which was ridiculous, given that she'd known him all of four and a half days and they'd spent most of that time in bed.

She focused on his driving instead. She'd never taken lessons, or a test, or even sat behind the wheel of a car. She was always in the back, being driven places, never driving there. Never choosing her destination or even her direction herself.

She wasn't now, either, she reminded herself. She had no idea where they were even going. She just hoped that Matteo did.

'There it is,' he said eventually, and Isabella forced herself to pay attention to her surroundings again, rather than just her thoughts. Here she was, in this most beautiful of locations, and she was—

'Wow!' She interrupted her own thoughts as she finally took in where they were headed.

There, jutting out over the water of Lake Geneva, was a castle—a proper, fairy-tale castle.

'I thought it might be rather old hat to you, living in a palace like you do,' Matteo said, with a grin.

She smiled back. 'Not one like this, though.'

The palace at Augusta was very grand, filled with tapestries and red brocade and family portraits and all the other things royals seemed to need to prove their place in the world. But the truth was the original palace had burnt almost to the ground in the late nineteenth century, and the rebuilt version, while beautiful, didn't have the history of a place like this. Or the magic.

'What's it called?' she asked, still wondering at the sight.

'Château de Chillon,' Matteo replied. 'Chillon Castle.'

Fat round turrets climbed towards the bright blue sky, joined by boxier square ones, many of them topped by flags that fluttered in the light summer breeze. She could imagine Rapunzel sitting at the top of one of them, her hair hanging out of the window just waiting for a prince to scamper up it and set her free.

'Do you want to go inside?' Matteo asked.

'Can we?' She felt her eyes widen. Only strictly arranged visits were allowed at the castle in Augusta, and Isabella had spent the last few years carefully avoiding any of them.

Matteo just smiled.

It turned out that tourists were welcome at the Château de Chillon, and nobody seemed to notice that one of the tourists was actually a visiting member of another royal family. Isabella kept her sunglasses on to hide her face, but, honestly, she didn't think anyone was looking at her anyway. The castle was full of enough treasures to draw attention away. From the open courtyards to the friezes painted on the walls— not to mention the views out over the lake and the mountains, or towards the vineyards.

'Besides,' Matteo murmured in her ear as they took in one of the displays of armour, 'who would honestly expect a real princess to be walking around with the rest of the tourists?'

After they'd toured the rooms of the castle that were open to them, they climbed to the top of the keep in the centre of the castle and took in the view all around them. Standing close behind her, Matteo whispered information about what they were looking at into her ear as he turned her to face different directions.

'And that, down there, is where I'm taking you tomorrow,' he said finally.

Isabella squinted to see where he was pointing. 'The Château café?'

Matteo shook his head. 'The town of Montreux.'

CHAPTER EIGHT

MATTEO WAS STILL grinning to himself as he showered the day off him and changed into loose trousers and a shirt for dinner on the balcony that evening. The trip to Château du Chillon had been a success, and Isabella had already all but agreed to another outing tomorrow.

'I'd never have seen this, if I hadn't met you,' she'd whispered to him, as they'd stood atop the keep tower, looking out over water and mountains and towns and fields. 'Thank you.'

He'd known then that he couldn't stop yet.

As much as he wanted to take Isabella to bed and keep her there for the rest of their stay at the villa, there was a certain joy in exploring their surroundings with her too. His favourite part was watching Isabella get to pretend to be a normal, ordinary person, rather than a princess. The pleasure she took from fading into the background and watching others—even when they were just sitting in the café together sipping coffee—was palpable.

I gave that to her. She'll remember that.

It was something, at least.

And, he thought as he headed out to meet her on the balcony, he was almost certain that their day trips into tourist life wouldn't be the only things she remembered. She'd remember the nights they had together, too—the same way he would.

Those nights were seared into his memory for ever, he knew that already.

'What's on the menu tonight?' Matteo's blood warmed at the sight of Isabella in another one of her sundresses. This one, he noted, tied around the neck, covering her high to her throat and down to her ankles. While it showed off her beautiful shoulders, it was definitely more modest than many of the others she'd worn.

Then she turned to get to what had become, over the past few days, her chair, and he saw that the whole back was missing, the fabric draping down over the swell of her bottom, so low that he was pretty sure there was no way she was wearing anything at all under the dress.

God, he hoped not. Even if he wasn't entirely sure how to get through dinner without knowing for sure.

Isabella lifted the metal cloche covering their plates and revealed a chicken dish with a creamy mushroom and leek sauce, plus a side dish of potatoes, and licked her lips in anticipation. Matteo's body tightened at the sight. He wanted her to look at him that way, and soon.

'I've been looking forward to this all day, haven't you?' she said. 'I'm starving. Not that the sandwich in the Château café wasn't lovely too…'

How were they still talking about food? When she looked like that and he hadn't touched her for *hours*.

Had he totally regressed to being a teenager, unable to think about anything but sex? Apparently so.

Then she looked up and met his gaze, and he watched her pupils widen further. Was she having the same thoughts that he was? It looked likely. And yet, decorum dictated that they eat dinner before anything else.

Matteo hated decorum. But despite all his efforts, Isabella was still ruled by it.

That, or she was just tormenting him for fun.

Dinner was an excruciatingly pleasurable torture. Every mouthful she took made him want to kiss her more. Each time she reached for her wine glass that damn dress shifted around what he was now certain were her bare breasts, and he ached to touch her.

Isabella kept up a light conversation about the château and the sights they'd enjoyed that day, seemingly unaware of his distraction, until she'd finished the last mouthful of her lemon mousse.

Then she smiled at him, warm and wicked, and he knew that every moment of the meal had been intentional.

'What shall we do with the rest of our evening, I wonder?' she said, her voice too innocent to be real. 'It's been such a lovely day, and we only have such a limited time here, it seems a shame to waste the later hours. We could walk by the lake, perhaps, or in the gardens. Or maybe there's another board game around here somewhere we could play…'

She started to stand, and Matteo's hand shot out to circle her wrist with firm fingers. 'Or I could take you to bed right now and see how loudly I can make you scream using only my tongue.'

Her pulse kicked up a gear under his fingertips, and he knew they weren't going to be playing Monopoly again any time soon.

'Or we could do that.' Isabella's eyes were nearly black as she slid into his lap, warm and wanting.

Matteo slid his hands up under the fabric of her skirt, palms against the smooth skin of her thighs. 'Was this whole meal just a plan to torture me?'

'Well, I was genuinely hungry.' She kissed his neck, and he shivered with need. 'But honestly? Yes.'

'Why?'

She shrugged, and everything moved under her dress in a way that made his everything stand even more firmly to attention. Any moment now, he was going to untie that tiny ribbon bow that held the dress up and let it fall away completely. Then he'd know for sure what was under it.

God, he hoped it was nothing but Isabella's bare skin.

'Because…you were in charge today,' she said. 'You drove, decided where we went, how long we stayed. And I loved our day out, I really did—and I wouldn't have had the courage to take us there myself, even if I *could* drive. But…'

'You wanted to be in charge of something too,' he guessed. 'In control.'

'I suppose so.' She shrugged again and he nearly lost his mind. 'Silly, really.'

'Not at all.' How often did a princess get to decide anything about her life? Not nearly often enough, was Matteo's guess. 'So, do you want to choose our activities for the rest of the week?'

She tilted her head a little as she studied him, and he realised he could look right down the side of her dress. *Definitely* no bra.

He'd let her decide everything if she'd just let him confirm the 'no underwear' part of his hypothesis.

'No,' she said finally. 'Not all of them. Just some of them.'

'That sounds fair.' He swallowed. 'So, do you want to play Monopoly, or…?'

Isabella reached up behind her neck and unfastened the bow that had been driving him crazy for the last hour. Then she stood up, let the dress fall to the floor of the balcony, and stalked naked back into her bedroom.

'We're definitely going with your plan for this evening,' she called back over one bare shoulder. 'What are you waiting for?'

Matteo hurried to his feet and after her.

They only had two more days, after all. He didn't want to waste a moment.

At the palace in Augusta, a week could feel like a year if there wasn't anything interesting going on—or, as often happened, if she was avoiding getting caught up in official royal engagements where her only purpose was to smile and stay quiet. Here on Lake Geneva, Isabella's week with Matteo seemed to have passed in a flash.

Which wasn't to say they hadn't made the most of their time together. Quite apart from the hours spent exploring each other's bodies, or whispering thoughts and histories to each other in the dark, Matteo had taken her on the sort of everyday adventures she'd never been allowed to have before.

He hadn't pushed her too far, ever, but just slipping away from their security detail—who'd been surprisingly sanguine about it after the first time, so she suspected Gianna had had a word and told them to let them go—felt like a rebellion. Putting on a floppy straw hat and wandering incognito around the resort town of Montreux, eating lunch in a side-street café where no one knew who she was, or even who Matteo was, had felt liberating. Swimming in the waters of Lake Geneva, with Matteo's arms around her as he stole wet kisses, had been something entirely new.

And then there were the nights.

After Nate, she'd never really expected to feel such passion again—or to trust it if she did. But with Matteo, everything seemed so natural. Whatever her body needed, he was always there to give it to her. And she felt no embarrassment in needing to learn what he liked, what he wanted, what made him moan and flip them over and thrust into her until they both fell over the edge of pleasure together.

Being with Matteo had felt nothing like her time with Nate. Nothing like anything she'd ever experienced before.

And now, too soon, it was time to say goodbye to it and head back to the real world.

They'd elected to spend their last day together at the villa—mostly in bed, which was fine by Isabella. The morning had been a haze of pleasure and the occasional pastry and coffee, when they needed to build up their energy reserves again. They'd managed a small walk down to the water's edge and along the path after lunch, but the temptation to touch and kiss and more had been too great, and it wasn't long before they were back in bed.

Maybe they were just reassuring each other that they were still there. For now. Isabella wasn't sure. She was trying to ignore the fact that, after tomorrow, she'd be on her own again.

'What are you thinking about?' Matteo murmured against her shoulder.

She twisted under the light sheets until she could rest her cheek against his chest. 'Tomorrow, I guess.'

Matteo was silent for a moment. 'Back to the

real world, huh? You going to miss me?' He grinned as he said it, and she knew it was just a joke, a request from his perfectly healthy ego.

'I'll miss *this*.' She pressed a kiss to his skin, then lifted her face to kiss his lips, too. 'This week…it's like I've been a different person. It's strange to think I have to say goodbye to her tomorrow morning.'

And to you.

'You've been able to be Isabella. Not just the Princess.'

'Yeah.' And now she wasn't sure she wanted to go back to being the Princess at all. But what choice did she have? It was who she was. Who her family expected her to be.

She'd always known that her place in the family, the love of the King, Queen and all their subjects, were contingent on following The Rules. Ever since she'd heard the whispered stories about her Aunt Josephine, and her banishment from the palace after she fell in love with the man who looked after her horses—old gossip by the time it had reached ten-year-old Isabella's ears, but still shocking. Aunt Josephine had refused to give him up, and that was why Isabella had never met her.

Everything that had happened with Nate had only reinforced the lesson and confirmed to her that nothing had changed. Augusta was still as rule-bound, stuffy and unforgiving as always.

Beside her, Matteo shifted, lying flat beside her on his side so he could meet her gaze. 'You told me that you'd taken time off from being a princess once before. But you never told me what happened.'

'No, I didn't.' And that had been intentional. She'd distracted him, got him to tell her his secrets instead. He'd shared about his brother's death, his bucket list, everything.

And she'd kept her secrets close, locked inside, as always.

'No one can ever know, Isabella.' Her father's words. And, always remembering Aunt Josephine, she'd lived by them.

'Will you tell me now?' Matteo asked.

Isabella bit her lip as she considered. Matteo wouldn't spill her secrets—if he was going to, he had far juicier stuff to share now after their week together. Plus, there was that non-disclosure agreement he must have signed before coming to Lake Geneva in the first place.

Besides, she knew in her heart that Matteo wouldn't betray her that way.

Except I thought the same thing about Nate, too.

Was that why she didn't want to tell him? No, she admitted to herself. It wasn't fear that was stopping her telling him the truth. It was shame, or at least embarrassment. That she'd ever been that naive, trusting girl.

That, in some ways, she still was.

'If you don't want to—' Matteo started, but she cut him off.

'No. I mean, yes, I don't. But not because of you. Because of me. Because it's just so…stupid.'

This wasn't like the secrets he'd shared with her. Nothing so tragic as a dead brother, or as noble as fulfilling his lost dreams. This was just…humiliating.

'Okay.' Matteo looked confused. She didn't really blame him.

With a sigh, she sat up, drawing the sheets up to cover her bare breasts. 'I'll tell you. But bring me some of those chocolates first, okay?' She was going to need something sweet to counteract the bitterness of the memory.

He flashed her an indulgent smile, then retrieved the box of truffles from the table in the corner, placing them on the bed between them as he settled back down next to her.

Isabella took one and stuffed it in her mouth as she figured out how best to begin.

'I've never told this story to anyone,' she said. 'The only people who know are the ones who lived it with me. So if I don't tell it well, that's why. Okay?'

'Okay.' Matteo wrapped an arm around her shoulders, pulling her closer. 'And if you want to stop, if you decide you don't want me to know, that's fine too, okay? I won't push.'

Another difference between him and Nate. Nate had *always* pushed. He'd had to, hadn't he? It was his job.

'When I was twenty-two, I met a guy.' God, how many tragic stories started that way? Too many, Isabella was sure. 'Nathanial was Augustan and from a decent enough family to be invited to an event at the palace, but not aristocracy, so not a suitable courtship partner for me in the eyes of my family. But I thought I was in love, of course. At his urging, I'd throw off my princess persona and escape the castle to be with him. He was my first love, my first everything really. Being with him was the first time since puberty that I felt like myself, like Isabella, not just a princess.'

'So, what went wrong?' Matteo asked. 'Your parents found out?'

'They did,' Isabella admitted. 'But not until it showed up in the papers. It turned out that Nate was an aspiring reporter, and he'd used his flirtation with me to get photos, quotes about my family, insider gossip from the palace, everything. He sold it to the *Augustan Times* in return for a job there.'

Matteo swore. 'Bella, I'm… That's awful. I'm so sorry.'

'It was a long time ago. Five years—no, nearly six since it started.' And in that whole time she'd kept her distance from everyone, kept herself safe behind the title of Princess, using it as a barrier. Until this week.

'What happened next?'

'Isn't that enough?' She flashed him a grin, but she could see from his eyes that he knew the aftermath mattered almost as much as the event itself. She sighed and went on. 'The palace put out a statement denying most of it—saying he was a desperate young man who had made up these quotes and stories to find fame. But there were photos of us together, and too many of the stories rang true with other gossip, so I don't think anyone believed it. It was easy enough to see what had really happened. I'd been a fool.'

Matteo shook his head. 'You were taken advantage of. You were in love.'

'I'm not even sure I was, now. Not really. Love…you think you know what it is when it happens for the first time, don't you? But now, I'm not sure I'd recognise it if it jumped up and down throwing heart confetti at me. I just… I don't know how anyone trusts anyone else that much. Not without a non-disclosure agreement, anyway.' She laughed at her joke, but he didn't.

'Isabella.' His bright green eyes were serious. 'You know I wouldn't tell anyone about all we've shared here this week, non-disclosure agreement or not.'

'I do.' She couldn't have explained how she knew she could trust him, but there was no doubt inside her that she did. She'd trusted him with her body all week. She could trust him with her secrets, too.

'Anyway, my parents—and my older brother, Leo—were all horrified at the peril I'd placed the palace in. Those are their exact words, incidentally.' She almost smiled at the memory, except to this day the sight of the King and Queen and the Crown Prince of Augusta all staring at her in disapproving disbelief was still the thing that gave her the most nightmares. 'They couldn't believe I hadn't seen what was happening. In fact… I wondered if they actually thought I'd done it on purpose, as some sort of rebellion.'

'Did you ever ask them that?'

Isabella shook her head. 'No. We…after all the initial lectures and lessons about how to guard my royal privacy—or, more pertinently, theirs—we never talked about it again. His name is never mentioned in the palace, neither is that whole period of my life. It's as if it never happened.' As if she'd never been anyone but Princess Isabella at all. Just as Aunt Josephine had been written out of the family history.

Matteo was silent for a long moment, his lips pressed against her hair. She could almost hear him thinking.

'Do you think…this week…?' he said, finally. 'Has it given you anything?'

She didn't have to think about the answer. 'It's given me everything.'

The chance to be herself, for once, not her title. The ability to explore all the things she'd never thought she'd have again. To take a few risks, to live a little.

But most of all, it had enabled her to trust her own judgement again. To believe that Isabella was a person worth being, princess or not.

She couldn't put all that emotion into words, though. Not without ugly crying, and ruining their last, perfect night together. So instead, she reached up and wound a hand around the back of Matteo's neck, pulling his mouth to hers, putting all of her feelings into her kisses instead.

And as he responded she knew that this was the perfect way to spend their final hours together. Lost in each other, bodies so close they were almost the same person, without any more secrets between them. Just enjoying this space out of time, where they could be themselves.

This is perfect, Isabella thought as Matteo made love to her, the intensity of their coupling somehow so much more than the other nights they'd spent together.

So close, as her body tightened and her release swelled within her, and Matteo began to move faster as she fought to match his pace.

So perfect, as her orgasm crashed over her, and every muscle in her body seemed to tense then relax, drifting away on a contented cloud of daydreams.

In fact, everything was perfect, until Matteo jumped up and swore, loudly and proficiently.

'What is it?' she asked, forcing her trembling body to sit up.

He met her gaze with grave eyes. 'The condom broke.'

CHAPTER NINE

THE NEXT MORNING—the last morning—Matteo sat on the balcony with his morning coffee and watched Isabella leave.

Except in reality she'd already left him, hours ago. The moment the damn condom broke, she'd shot out of his bed and his life.

He'd tried to talk to her, of course. Offered to find the nearest all-night chemist that might provide a morning-after pill or something, but she'd refused to listen. Told him she'd handle it herself.

Which he expected meant she'd be asking one of her royal advisors to handle it, since he couldn't exactly see her walking into a pharmacy herself to do it.

But after all the walls they'd broken down between them over the past week, it frustrated the hell out of him that this had put them all back up again.

She hadn't even joined him for breakfast that

morning—which meant she hadn't eaten anything at all. Behaviour so unlike the Isabella he'd come to know this week, he'd really started to worry.

She had come to say goodbye, though. He supposed that much politeness at least was bred into princesses.

'My assistant will be here with my car any moment,' she'd said, lingering in the doorway to the balcony. 'I'm going to go and wait downstairs. So… I guess this is goodbye.'

'I'll take your bag down for you,' he'd offered, but she'd shaken her head.

'Even princesses can carry a bag, Matteo.' It had been a joke, he supposed, but he hadn't laughed.

Because that was what she was again, wasn't it? Princess Isabella, a world away from him.

And because of a stupid piece of latex, he hadn't even been able to enjoy their last night together.

'It's too much, Matteo,' she'd whispered through the door, after she'd shut it on him. *'Too much risk. This whole week… It's too much.'*

She wasn't wrong. He'd spent a sleepless night trying to deal with just how much it all was. And how saying goodbye suddenly seemed so much bigger than it had in his head, now he really had to do it.

He wasn't a fool. He hadn't expected this week to end with hearts and flowers and a royal wedding, even before she'd told him about her experiences with the idiot reporter. And he hadn't wanted it to, either.

Matteo Rossi wasn't the settling-down type, and he definitely wasn't anybody's idea of a prince.

But the idea of never seeing Isabella again—never touching her, never kissing her, never making love to her again—that made his whole chest ache in a way he hadn't anticipated when he'd stood on this balcony a week ago and looked down to see her standing on the terrace.

Maybe M knew what it was doing after all. Because he'd never met a woman so perfect for him.

If only she weren't the most impossible person for him to love, all at the same time.

This was for the best. He had to remember that. He needed to live his own life, a life he couldn't live if he was worrying about her—or even if he knew she was somewhere, worrying about him. Love, like the love he'd felt for his mother and brother, came with limits, and it came with loss and pain.

He didn't have space for any of those things

in the life he was living for himself, and for Giovanni.

A car pulled around the corner of the driveway, out from the trees that shielded the villa from the passing roads, and halted beside the terrace. Tinted windows, probably bullet-proof glass, and high wheels that put the driver and passengers above many of the other cars on the road.

A carriage fit for a princess—a modern-day one, anyway. Even if Augusta seemed to be stuck in the past when it came to the rules it expected its princesses to follow.

The honey-blonde woman Isabella had been arguing with the day he first saw her—Gianna, his memory filled in—stepped out from the back seat and hurried across to the terrace. Just like that first day, he was too far away to make out their conversation, but the concern on Gianna's face was evident even at a distance. What did she see in Isabella's face that made her look like that?

He wished he knew. That he could see. That he could take the Princess in his arms and kiss her better.

Was Isabella feeling as torn up as he was right now? Or was she just telling her friend about last night's accident and begging her to help make it go away.

His child…

No. That was stupid. It was one broken condom; the chances of Isabella being pregnant were low, surely?

Just imagining it was another way to hold onto her, beyond the end of this week. And that wasn't something he could do; they'd both been clear enough about that from the start. Nothing had changed in either of their worlds outside this place.

Even if he felt like a different person inside, all of a sudden.

Down on the terrace, Gianna put her arm around Isabella and led her towards the car, carrying her case in her other hand. Matteo watched intently from the balcony. Would she turn around? Would she wave goodbye? Did he even want her to? He wasn't sure.

Isabella reached the car door, and he braced himself for her disappearing behind those tinted windows, and the prison of her position as Princess. But, at the last minute, she paused and looked back up at him.

He drank in that last glimpse of her. That creamy skin, the dark curls that bounced past her shoulders. The curves he'd held close. The lips he'd kissed.

She raised her hand, a last royal wave. He

huffed a laugh he knew she'd never hear and blew her a kiss instead.

And then, with the closing of a door and the purr of an engine, Princess Isabella of Augusta drove out of his life for good.

'Are you really sure you're okay?' Gianna asked as the car door shut behind her, and the driver started the engine again. 'I thought you were having fun! When you texted, you said it was good, that he was nice.'

Her head was buzzing with all the things she'd never said to him. With the memory of that awful moment last night. With the fear and the risk that had sent her running from his arms.

'I'm fine,' Isabella lied. 'Really.'

Gianna clearly didn't believe her. She reached across the seat between them and took the Princess's hand in her own. 'If he did something, said something, you need to tell me now, Your Highness. He signed a non-disclosure agreement, so we can sue him to high heaven if he tries to sell his story, but if there's anything more—'

Isabella sobbed a laugh. 'No! No, honestly, Gianna. It's nothing like that. He was…he was wonderful.'

And she'd run out on him, too afraid to face the risks she'd been taking.

No birth control was one hundred per cent effective, she knew that. There was always the risk of pregnancy, from the moment she'd decided to take him to bed.

She'd told herself that it was Matteo making her take more risks—ditching the security detail, swimming in the lake, pretending to be a normal tourist—but she'd taken the biggest one all by herself. She'd let him into her bed, into her body.

Even *that* wasn't the biggest risk she'd taken this week, even if the magnitude of what she'd done was only now crashing down on her as she drove away.

She'd let him into her *heart*.

And now she wasn't entirely sure how to get him back out again. If that was even possible.

Was this how Aunt Josephine felt?

Gianna's expression had gone from concerned to horrified. 'I should never have sent you. Oh, Your Highness, I'm so sorry! It was meant to be fun, a chance for you to relax...'

'It was all those things,' Isabella sobbed. 'Honestly, I'm glad you set it up.' Even if now she couldn't stop crying.

'Isabella, what *happened*?' Gianna asked, desperately, and Isabella knew her friend had to be worried because she'd used her name, not her title.

'I don't know,' Isabella replied. There were still tears dripping down her face; she could feel them plopping off her chin and nose and into her lap. God, she was a mess. 'I don't know.'

I'm very afraid I might have started to fall in love. And I might be pregnant. And both of these things are impossible, and no one can ever know.

Matteo hadn't wanted a perfect-match love affair any more than she had at the start of the week, and she had no reason to believe his feelings on that had changed. They were from two different worlds, and they both wanted to stay in them. Love was off the table.

She should ask Gianna to take them by a pharmacy, or to call the royal family doctor, or something. She needed to do something about that burst condom.

This wasn't just an ill-advised affair. This wasn't an immature fling gone wrong. It wasn't some photos and embarrassing quotes in the paper.

A princess, pregnant out of wedlock? A single-mother princess?

Augusta was a conservative country, and its monarchs were the most conservative of all. Her parents might never get over the shock.

They'd forgiven her once, for being young and stupid. They'd blamed her naivety, given her the benefit of the doubt and helped her cover it up. Hammered home The Rules to make sure she couldn't make the same mistake twice.

But she wasn't so young now, and she didn't feel stupid, or as if her time with Matteo was a mistake. Would they forgive her again? Or would this be one transgression too far?

She should make sure she didn't put them in the position of having to decide.

She should.

But instead, she hugged herself and cried. For the life she'd had a glimpse of, the possibilities she'd walked away from, and the future she knew could never be hers.

He wasn't back on the team.

Matteo had left Lake Geneva for Rome, ready to throw himself back into his normal life, only to discover that his normal life wasn't ready for him yet.

'That leg needs another few weeks of physio,' Gabe told him on his return. 'Doctor's orders— don't blame me.'

He did, of course. He blamed everybody there for messing with his career, his head, his future.

For showing him something he couldn't

have. Something he'd never even imagined he might want, until now.

So now he was sitting in Gabe's office—feet on the desk, of course—figuring out his next move.

'You do realise you don't have to be here, don't you?' Gabe said as he walked in, a sheaf of papers in his hands.

'I'm still part of the team, aren't I?' Matteo said obstinately. 'Even if I'm not allowed to race.'

Gabe rolled his eyes. 'You're on medical leave, Matteo.' He moved to push Matteo's feet from the desk before obviously remembering about his still-healing leg and resisting the urge.

Matteo kept his feet exactly where they were. 'My leg is fine,' he grumbled.

'Then you can get it off my desk.'

Rolling his eyes, Matteo stomped his feet onto the ground. 'Look, if I was well enough to be shipped off to Lake Geneva to show some random woman the sights, I'm well enough to drive, yeah?'

Taking his own seat on the other side of the desk, Gabe looked at him with interest. 'I've been waiting to hear all about your Swiss exploits. Are you ready to share with Uncle Gabe yet?'

Matteo shrugged. 'What's to share? It was a

week in Lake Geneva taking in the tourist at-
tractions and eating too much good food.'

'With a woman that M dating agency swears
is your perfect match.' From the smirk on
Gabe's face, he could tell that his manager
wasn't taking that claim any more seriously
than Matteo had, when he'd arrived at the villa.

Before he'd met Isabella.

'So, are you going to tell me about her?'
Gabe pushed.

'What do you want to know?' Suddenly, he
was strangely reluctant to share any details of
his week. To give up any of the perfect, private experience that had been his week with
Isabella.

The memories were his, and they were hers,
and they didn't belong to anyone else.

Even when Madison Morgan herself had
called to check in, post-date-week, and ask how
it had gone, Matteo had kept his responses to
a minimum. He'd confirmed that they'd had a
great time, that the villa was perfect and they'd
got on well, but left it at that. Madison had
sounded faintly disappointed, but she was a
professional, and she hadn't pushed him for
gossip or sordid details.

Gabe, Matteo knew from experience, would
definitely push him for both of those things.

'Was she as perfect for you as the agency promised?' Gabe asked, surprising him.

'Yes.' The word was out before he could stop it. 'In lots of ways, she was.'

Gabe beamed like a proud father. 'So, you'll be seeing her again?'

Matteo shook his head. 'I don't imagine so.'

'Why not?'

Gabe, Matteo knew, had been married to the love of his life since he was twenty-two, and never looked at another woman. He lived vicariously through his drivers, instead. For him, love was simple: you found it, you grabbed it, and you made damn sure never to let go.

He wouldn't understand that Isabella wasn't meant for him to hold onto, even if he wanted to.

What Isabella needed most in the world was to fly free; but what her position demanded of her was the opposite. That wasn't a fight Matteo intended to get in the middle of—not when she'd so clearly already made her choice.

'It wouldn't work between us,' Matteo said eventually. It had the benefit of being true, at least.

'How can you know if you don't try?'

When he didn't answer, Gabe sighed, and tossed the paperwork he clearly wasn't reading aside on his desk. Matteo wondered if he had enough time to run before the inevitable lecture Gabe was obviously building up to.

'Matteo…' Apparently not. 'You know I love you like a younger brother. A son, even.'

'Right down to the parental lectures and interfering in my love life, apparently.'

'You haven't *had* a love life until now,' Gabe pointed out. 'A sex life, sure. A dating life, for definite. But love?'

'I'm not looking for love,' Matteo pointed out.

'Why not?'

Because if I can't have Isabella, what's the point?

'Because love would slow me down.' That was a more acceptable, Matteo Rossi answer, right? 'You know how it goes. You fall in love and suddenly you have to change your whole life for them. Be more careful—on the track and off. Stop doing fun stuff.'

'*Dangerous* stuff,' Gabe countered.

'The stuff that makes me feel like I'm *living*.' Except he'd felt alive with Isabella. Calm, at peace—but alive. And now he'd crossed off everything on Giovanni's list, what was he going to do next, anyway? What risks were still out there to take? What heart-pulsing, blood-pumping things could he do to make the most of his life?

Possibly getting a princess pregnant is probably pretty risky, his mind added unhelpfully. *Her parents could probably have me assassinated.*

Okay, he wasn't thinking about that any more. Wasn't thinking about Isabella, either. Because whatever he thought he might have to give up for a chance of a relationship with her, it was nothing to what she would definitely have to sacrifice. Augustan princesses couldn't fall in love with Italian racing-car drivers. It was aristocracy or nothing.

He'd done a little research since he left Lake Geneva—and not just to look at photos of Isabella online, and curse the fact that he hadn't had the foresight to take any of her while they were together, if she'd have even let him. He'd found, buried in the depths of the Internet, the original coverage of the debacle she'd told him about with the reporter. And, with it, an interesting sidebar about the traditions of royal marriage in Augusta.

She'd have to give up her title, her place in the line of succession, not to mention probably a lot of money, to marry someone her family didn't approve of. Apparently her aunt had made the sacrifice before Isabella was even born. Augustan royalty took the rules seriously. No wonder she didn't want to chance getting close to anyone that might make her want to risk it.

Across the desk, Gabe was watching him silently, as if he could see Matteo's thoughts ticking across his brain. Matteo sincerely hoped that he couldn't, for any number of reasons.

'I'm not going to tell you that life without love isn't worth living,' he said slowly. 'But I would like you to think about one thing, Matteo. Will you do that for me?'

'Of course.' Gabe had been his mentor as much as his manager for most of his adult life. He always thought about the things Gabe told him—even though most often they were to do with how he took a corner, or the right mindset for an upcoming race.

'All the things you've done—the places you've been, the adventures you've had—you've done them alone. Ever since Giovanni died, it's just been you against the world, and every challenge it can throw at you.' Gabe got to his feet, the papers he'd walked in with long forgotten. 'Wouldn't it be nice to have someone to face those challenges with, again?'

He left before Matteo could marshal any arguments against his words, or point out that no one would ever be able to take his brother's place in his heart.

And as the door swung shut behind him

Matteo used the sound of it crashing closed to ignore the voice inside his head that whispered: *Not replacing. Something new.*

Was it time for something new? Not Isabella, not love—there were still too many reasons that Gabe didn't understand why that wasn't an option.

But he'd completed Giovanni's list. He'd done everything his brother had ever dreamed of.

He was done. And that revelation felt like a weight off his shoulders, as if he were flying again, rather than held down by reality.

For so many years, ever since he'd made his promise to Giovanni, he'd been living by someone else's beliefs, following someone else's dreams. And it had brought him so far, given him so much, he couldn't regret it—especially not when he knew what it would have meant to his brother.

But still…

Now he had fulfilled his promise, that meant it was time for Matteo to live by his own beliefs, follow his own dreams. Set his own challenges and meet them.

Once he figured out what they should be.

He needed new adventures. Bigger, riskier ones. He needed to take life to the edge.

That was what he'd done when Giovanni died: filled the gaping hole where his brother had been with experiences. With reminders of everything the world had to offer.

With proof that he, at least, was still alive.

He needed to do the same thing again now. That was all.

Lost in thought, he reached across the desk to grab a blank piece of printer paper and a pen and started to write.

CHAPTER TEN

A WEEK LATER, Isabella stared at the diary on the desk in front of her and sighed.

'What's with the sighing?' Gianna peered over her shoulder at the blank boxes. 'It's a quiet week. I thought you'd be pleased.'

'I am. Mostly.' Her weeks at the palace didn't tend to be busy anyway, given her aversion to public events. But sometimes things snuck into her calendar when she wasn't there to stop them, and a few had definitely been added to her future diary while she was away in Switzerland. She'd struggled through the ones in her first week back and was already thinking of ways to get out of most of the others, even though they were weeks away.

But she'd asked for a quiet week this week, and she'd got it.

Except now she had no idea what to do with the free time.

Sitting alone with her thoughts simply wasn't

an option, because her thoughts all revolved around one thing. Well, two, technically, although they both linked back to the same man.

Number one: she missed Matteo, with the kind of ache she'd never felt for Nate.

Number two: her period was late. Four days late, to be precise, since she should have had it a week after her return from Switzerland.

She didn't need it circled in red in her official engagements diary or anything to know that; she'd been counting the days ever since she left Lake Geneva. Her period was normally like clockwork—the same as her schedule. She'd have assumed Gianna had organised it like the rest of her life, except that Gianna was all about Isabella's public persona, and nobody in Augusta wanted to think about the royals having bodily functions like that, surely?

Matteo had urged her to take risks, to get out there and live life while she had the chance, in Switzerland. But she was pretty sure he didn't mean this kind of risk.

Gianna was perched on the desk beside her, looking down at Isabella with concern.

'Is it still…him?' she asked softly. 'You're thinking about him again?'

'Yes.' There was no point lying about it. While she'd tried to keep the details about her time at the villa to a minimum, Gianna had organised the whole thing. She knew why she'd been there, and she'd seen the state she was in upon leaving.

'I should never have sent you there,' Gianna said now, shaking her head sadly. 'I never thought… I know they claim to find a perfect match, but I never imagined you could fall like this in just one week.'

Isabella looked up sharply. *A fallen woman.* How did she know? 'What do you mean? Fall?'

'In love,' Gianna replied. Her eyes were pitying. 'Your Highness, you have to believe I'd never have sent you there if I really thought you were going to fall in love. Not with someone you can't be with.'

'I'm not in love.' She wasn't. *But I could be.* If she let herself fall, let herself spend more time with Matteo…she knew in her heart he was someone she could love, for real this time.

She just wouldn't let herself, because what good would that do them?

'Isabella—'

'You said it yourself,' she said sharply, cutting off her friend. 'Who falls in love in a week? Besides, whatever M claim, how could they find my perfect match without knowing the truth of who I am? You filled in those forms for me, and I didn't even know what that video interview was for. And since Matteo was in hospital with a broken leg when his application went in, I don't even think he did it all himself either. He said his manager set it up for him to keep him out of trouble.'

Gianna looked sceptical, but she didn't push it. Well, not too far. 'But you're still thinking about him.'

And the possibility he knocked me up.

She was going to have to talk to him, and soon. He deserved to know what was going on—and she could do with someone else to freak out about it with. If she told Gianna…her assistant was a friend, but she was also a royal employee. If she knew that the Princess was pregnant out of wedlock…and without even a romantic story to tell beyond a week-long Swiss booty call…she'd be obliged to tell the King and Queen.

Which was the absolute last thing that Isabella wanted.

Of course, then she'd have to confess her own part in the whole plan, Isabella supposed, but she liked Gianna too much to let her take the fall for that, anyway. No one had pushed her into Matteo's arms, or his bed. In fact, she'd stripped off in front of him and run there herself.

God, this was so much worse than anything Aunt Josephine had done. Especially if there was a baby…

She shook her head and forced a smile for Gianna. 'Well, then, I guess I need something to take my mind off things, don't you think? There must be something fun going on here at the palace, or some sort of royal trip that could benefit from a little bit of princessy sparkle, right?'

Anything to stop her wondering what would have happened if she hadn't run out on Matteo that last night. If they'd actually talked about what happened when they went back to reality, instead of trying to pretend it wasn't happening until the last minute.

If she was surprised at Isabella's sudden—and mostly unprecedented—interest in palace events, Gianna didn't show it. Probably because she knew how much she needed the distraction.

Instead, her assistant flipped through the giant paper organiser she insisted on using, even though the palace had invested in the latest technology for such things. 'There's a tea party for some of the country's most successful charitable fundraisers in the rose garden on Thursday. A visit from Augusta's greatest living novelist—'

Isabella groaned. 'Again? Why can't he just stay home and write more books?' She liked his novels far more than his company, and he always seemed to try and sit next to her at formal dinner, especially since he'd been appointed the Royal Writer last year. 'I definitely need something to get me away from the palace if he's visiting.'

'Well, Prince Leo is taking a trip to Rome at the weekend for a charity ball, if you *really* want to get away?'

Rome. 'Really?' She hadn't told Gianna that Matteo was Italian. Or that, according to his social media accounts—which she was only stalking under an anonymous account—he lived in Rome. Was there right now, in fact.

Why call, when she could talk to him face to face?

'Want me to ask your brother if there's space for one more on the trip?' Gianna asked, looking thrilled to have found something that distracted Isabella from her mysterious lover.

If only she knew...

'Well, I have been meaning to practise my Italian,' she said nonchalantly. 'Why don't you set it up, and I'll see if I have anything suitable to wear for a ball?'

And for seeing Matteo again, she hoped.

Matteo didn't know how Gabe talked him into stuff like this.

He was a racing driver, not some sort of wannabe philanthropist actor. Sure, he did what

he could for causes that mattered to him—
especially the cancer charity that had helped
Giovanni in his last days. Most of his riskiest
adventures were sponsored to raise money for
them. But that was the point, wasn't it? He liked
doing things for charity.

Showing up at some fancy ball in a tux and
having his photo taken a lot really didn't count.

Still, it *was* for charity, and Gabe was right
that his face was the most recognisable on the
team. So Matteo had put on his tux jacket and
bow tie and his best celeb smile and prepared
himself for a dull evening.

If he'd seen the guest list earlier, he'd have
known it would be anything but, he realised belatedly as a tall man with coal-black hair and
dark eyes entered the room followed by a whole
retinue and was announced.

'His Royal Highness Leonardo, the Crown
Prince of Augusta.'

Matteo's chest tightened. So this was Isabella's brother, Leo.

There was no reason to think that he'd have
brought his sister with him, but Matteo couldn't
stop himself craning around to see if there was
another royal hiding behind the Prince.

'Looking for someone?' Gabe asked, sounding amused.

It occurred to Matteo rather too late that his

manager, in setting up the whole 'perfect week in paradise' thing, had probably got to see a lot of the paperwork, before and after the trip. Including the name of Matteo's perfect match.

Damn.

'Her Highness Princess Isabella of Augusta.'

Matteo's heart stopped at the herald's words, and he ceased caring about what Gabe knew or didn't know. Instead, he turned to face the doorway full on, and tried to remember how to breathe as Isabella walked through it.

She's here. She's really here.

He'd honestly thought he might never be in the same room as her again, and now here she was.

Her ball gown, a deep midnight blue, sparkled under the lights of the ballroom, caressing her curves as he wanted to do. Her dark curls were piled on the top of her head, the creamy skin of her neck and shoulders bare except for the glint of sapphires, and her lips red and kissable.

She looked every inch the Princess, and Matteo wanted her so much he could hardly breathe.

As he watched she surveyed the room, chin held high and her gaze cool and assessing. Her manner was as many light years away from the relaxing, laughing, smiling, *touching* Isabella he'd spent the week with as her ball gown was from the light sundresses she'd worn there.

Then her gaze landed on him, and he saw the Isabella he'd fallen for in Switzerland behind all of her jewels and her title.

If she was surprised to see him, she didn't show it. But her gaze turned warmer, and he felt his body respond to her smile the way it always did.

Then her brother motioned to her, and she turned away to follow him as he toured the room, being introduced to the rich and charitable gathered in Rome for the occasion.

Matteo knew he should be circulating too, having the sort of conversations that led to donations, or someone offering him the opportunity to go and risk his neck to raise money for causes that mattered to him. But it was hard to concentrate on anything except the Princess in the room. Gabe, obviously aware of his distraction, covered for him in most of their conversations, and Matteo made a mental note to thank him later, when he wasn't so distracted.

Eventually, though, the Crown Prince had been introduced to and conversed with all the people who actually mattered in the ballroom and, as the orchestra struck up again after a break in the entertainment, and people began to flood back onto the dance floor, Leo and Isabella finally reached Matteo and Gabe.

'Your Royal Highnesses,' their guide said, 'may I introduce Mr Matteo Rossi, the current world champion racing driver, and his team manager, Mr Gabriel Esposito.'

The Crown Prince probably said something, but whatever it was Matteo didn't hear it. Not when he was taking Isabella's hand in his and lifting it to his lips, kissing it and wishing he could hold on for ever.

Never mind cliff diving, bungee jumping or jungle trekking. Seeing Isabella again made him feel more whole than any of those risky adventures ever had.

Gabe, as so many times before, was his saviour. In seconds flat he'd diverted Isabella's brother with a deep and meaningful conversation about something or other, guiding the Crown Prince's attention away from his sister and the racing driver she had supposedly just met.

'Do you dance, Mr Rossi?' Isabella asked, her voice a touch more formal than he was used to. He'd *never* been Mr Rossi to her before.

'I can try,' he said honestly. Because while his mother might have instilled good manners in her boys, dance lessons hadn't exactly been included.

Isabella flashed him a smile that made her look much more like the woman he knew and wanted. 'Just follow my lead.'

'Anywhere you want to go,' he replied.

Because if it meant being with Isabella tonight, he'd follow her into hell.

Matteo might be fast on his feet when chasing her to the bedroom, but he was not a born dancer. Not that it mattered to Isabella, since dancing together was nothing more than an excuse to get him alone—and lead him away from Leo.

Oh, and maybe an excuse to have him hold her again. She definitely wasn't overlooking the benefits of that.

He knew where to put his hands, at least, and Isabella managed to half dance, half drag him across the dance floor, towards the balcony she'd spotted on an earlier tour of the room. If she was lucky, it would be empty—but even if not, it would still be dark and more private than a crowded ballroom with all eyes on her. And besides, they'd always had good luck with balconies.

'I didn't expect to see you again,' Matteo murmured as they attempted a sort of waltz. She half expected him to add 'so soon', but he didn't, and it made his words sit all the heavier in her heart. He hadn't expected to see her at all. He'd expected that they'd both go their separate ways and that would be it.

Was that what he wanted? She'd never know if she didn't ask. And she *had* to know, before she told him about the apparent consequences of their week together.

'Disappointed?' she asked, as lightly as she could.

'Amazed. And thrilled.' His hand at her waist gripped her tighter. 'And a little hopeful.'

That made her smile—even though she wasn't sure how his mood might change when she told him why she was here.

'I was surprised to find it so easy to see you,' she admitted. 'When I found out Leo was coming to Rome, I tagged along in the hope of finding you. But I hardly expected you to show up at an event on my first night in town.'

'Fate, perhaps,' Matteo said. 'Or luck. Or maybe M had it right with that soulmates thing…'

'You think we'll keep being drawn together for ever, now we've met?' They'd reached the balcony, at last, and stopped dancing. Isabella raised an eyebrow as she waited for his answer.

In a moment, she'd open the door and lead him outside and tell him that she might be pregnant. For these last few seconds, she just wanted to enjoy being the way they'd been together in Lake Geneva.

'I think I wouldn't complain if we were.'

'Good answer.' Because there was a solid chance they were bound together for life, now, by a small cluster of cells growing inside her womb.

Moving out of his arms, she reached for the door handle to the balcony and pushed it open. She glanced around the ballroom, ascertaining that Leo was still fully occupied in conversation with Matteo's manager, and a few other guests who had joined them, and was unlikely to notice her absence for a while.

'Come on,' she said, dragging him with her into the cooler evening air of the balcony. He followed easily, shutting the door silently behind them.

They were lucky; the balcony was deserted. Isabella let out a long, relieved breath, as she moved away from the ballroom and to the stone and metal barrier at the edge of the balcony.

Matteo moved behind her, his whole body pressed up against hers as they looked out over the city below them—ancient and modern by turn, lit up by the moon and the yellow streetlights as the summer evening passed into darkness. She could see the curve of the Coliseum in the distance, the remains of Trajan's market beyond. Traffic and chatter and laughter hung in the air; the city was very much still awake, despite the hour.

It was late. She'd been travelling all day, then rushed to prepare for the ball that night, and then she'd been introduced to so many people her head was spinning with names and information, not to mention the worries she'd brought with her. She was exhausted.

But when she stood with Matteo at her back, when she felt his warmth through her ball gown, his kiss against the bare skin of her neck, above her mother's sapphire necklace... all of that faded away.

She forgot about Leo, inside, probably wondering where she was. She pushed out of her mind the reason she'd come to Rome. And instead, she relaxed against her lover, and let him carry the weight of all her thoughts for a while.

Matteo, for his part, seemed content to stand in silence with her, just enjoying their closeness. Every few moments he'd press a kiss to her hair, her throat, even the swell of her breast over her ball gown. But that was enough.

Until, apparently, it wasn't.

'Isabella,' he murmured against her ear. 'Why did you come to Rome?'

Because I might be pregnant.

The truth, but not all of it. There was another

truth she wanted him to know, too. So she gave him that, instead.

'Because I missed you.'

Matteo spun her round, pulling her tight against his chest as he kissed her soundly.

'You missed me too?' She laughed as he finally broke the kiss.

'More than I like to admit.' The truth of it was there in his eyes as she met his gaze.

She needed to tell him. And she would.

Just not yet.

Was it so wrong to want to enjoy this reunion just a little longer? To recapture everything she'd loved about being with him in Switzerland, before their situation got a lot more complicated?

'I dreamed about you,' she murmured, and watched his green eyes darken.

'Yeah? What did you dream?' His voice was gravelly and low, and it made her ache for him to touch her more.

'I dreamt of your hands on me.' At her words, Matteo slid his hands up from her waist, up to her breasts, rubbing his thumbs across her nipples through the thick fabric of her ball gown.

It wasn't enough; the fabric was too thick, she couldn't get the touch she needed. She whimpered her need to him, and it seemed Matteo understood. Without warning, he tugged it down just a couple of centimetres. Just enough to release her aching nipples. This time, when he brushed his thumbs across them, she moaned.

God, she hoped the music inside the ball-room was loud enough that no one heard her and came out to investigate.

'What else did you dream of?' Matteo's voice was rough with need, and Isabella thought longingly of the balcony at the villa in Lake Geneva, and how it conveniently led right to their bedrooms.

'Your mouth.' The words came out as a gasp, and Matteo flashed her a wicked smile before dipping his head lower.

His lips wrapped around first one nipple, then the other, giving each enough attention to make her squirm in his embrace.

'Anything else?' he asked, against her skin.

Time for some payback. Her hand snuck down to the front of his tuxedo trousers and pressed against the hardness she found there. 'I definitely dreamt about this, too. Inside me.'

Now it was Matteo's turn to let out a groan. 'Trust me, if I thought I could get away with making love to a princess here on a balcony, with the whole of Rome watching, I would.'

'Too much risk even for you, huh?' Isabella's

smile faltered as she remembered what other risks they'd taken.

'Maybe I'm just worried I couldn't make it good enough for you, up here,' Matteo countered.

'I doubt that. You managed fine on the balcony in Lake Geneva.'

'True.' Matteo's smile turned wicked. 'Want to find out if I still have the magic touch?'

God, she did. So much.

But her real reasons for being in Rome were too heavy in her mind—not to mention the risk of Leo coming out here to find her. That would be the end of her royal reputation for good.

She stepped away, tugging her dress back into position, as Matteo watched her, his eyes suddenly wary. And she knew she wouldn't be able to hide the truth from him any longer.

'Isabella, I'm going to ask you again. Why did you come to Rome?'

CHAPTER ELEVEN

MATTEO WASN'T ONE hundred per cent sure what the feeling thrumming through his body was, but he suspected it might be dread. Isabella bit down on her lower lip as she looked up at him, her warm brown eyes wide and guileless.

'I think I might be pregnant.'

All the dread that was bubbling through him gathered in his stomach, sinking it like a stone.

Pregnant. She might be pregnant. With his baby.

That last night. The broken condom. The risk that was so much greater than all the others he'd taken before.

Seeing Isabella again here in Rome…for a moment, he'd let himself get carried away, as he'd been able to do in Switzerland when it was just the two of them. For all of his protestations, he probably *would* have made love to her right there on the balcony if she'd let him.

She was a risk on a different level from any

skydive or impossible climb. The Crown Prince could probably get him arrested, and if someone down below had spotted them and the Rome *polizia* were called, he'd *definitely* have been spending the night in the cells.

And yet she was a risk he couldn't resist. Not for the adrenaline, like all the others. Just for her.

He'd made a lifestyle of outrunning risk, of beating all the odds, every time.

But this time, it looked as if it had caught up with him.

'We need to get you back in there before you're missed.' He brushed down the back of her ball gown and hoped that no one would notice any specks of balcony dirt in amongst the embroidery and the sparkly bits. Her lipstick was mostly gone, but hopefully she could replace that. And he'd managed not to muss up her hair too much.

'Matteo, we need to talk about this.'

'I know! I know. And I want to. Just…' The door to the balcony opened for a brief moment, a laughing couple audible in the gap, until they obviously realised the space was occupied and closed the door again to seek another spot for privacy. 'Not here,' Matteo finished, redundantly.

'Okay.' She didn't look happy about it, but at least she seemed to understand.

He hoped so. It wasn't that he didn't want to discuss the situation. He just needed to get his head around it a bit first.

Having a baby *definitely* wasn't on his list of adventures. But it seemed that someone else was writing his bucket list, once again.

'I wish we had more time,' he said. 'How long are you in Rome for?'

'Another few days. Come and find me at my hotel tomorrow?' she suggested. 'You can show me the sights of Rome. And we can talk.'

She wanted to escape her security *and* her brother in a strange city, with him? He'd taught her the fun of taking risks well, it seemed.

'I will,' he promised. He knew he wouldn't be able to stay away, not as long as he knew Isabella was so close. 'But we need to get back in there now.'

The thought of leaving her, of having to deal with all this, was making him shake. He stumbled, his hand slipping on the door handle until it opened, and the sounds of the ballroom surrounded them.

'We'll…we'll talk tomorrow, yeah?' he managed, as he staggered back into the room. 'Wait here, then follow me in a few minutes. Okay?'

Isabella nodded, but he could see the fear in her eyes, even in the dim lights.

Matteo shut the door behind him and walked

away. He needed to get away from the balcony before Isabella came out. He needed to be someone unsuspicious. To look as if he were having a perfectly ordinary evening—and his entire world hadn't been turned upside down.

He scanned the ballroom until he found Gabe—a solid, fixed point in his suddenly reeling world.

Gabe was a good manager and a better friend. While Matteo had no doubt Gabe knew where they were and what they were doing, he'd managed to keep Isabella's brother away from the balcony, holding him in conversation with a variety of people Matteo recognised by sight.

That was good. Taking off in the other direction, he headed for the bar, and a drink—making sure to keep the door to the balcony in his line of sight as much as he could. Leaning back against the bar, he watched Isabella reappear, slightly mussed, but still the most beautiful woman he'd ever seen. He saw the moment her brother spotted her and excused himself from Gabe. He saw Gabe clock Matteo on the other side of the room before he let him go.

And he heard the conversation between the royal siblings as they passed by him, heading towards the rest of their entourage.

'I just needed some air, Leo, that was all,' Isabella said. But her eyes met his for a moment, and he couldn't stop his smile. Even with everything, just looking at his Princess made his day better.

Luckily, the Crown Prince was oblivious to his presence. But not his existence.

'I was starting to worry you'd run off somewhere with that racing driver,' Leo joked. 'Honestly, Bella, we really do need to stick together at these things. Who knows? I might want to introduce you to someone you might find… suitable.'

The emphasis on 'suitable' was almost innuendo, and Matteo's grip on his glass tightened at the sound of it.

Of course, *he* wasn't suitable for a princess. He'd known that from the start.

But that didn't change the fact that she might just be carrying his baby. And that as terrifying as that was…it didn't feel like the end of the world.

Matteo threw back the whisky in his glass and wondered how long he had to wait before he could get out of there.

And how long before he could steal Isabella away again, to start figuring out what the hell they did next.

Oh, he really hadn't ever prepared for *this* sort of risk. But as long as they figured it out together…maybe it would be okay.

* * *

Isabella didn't sleep that night.

She wished she'd managed to slip Matteo her mobile number, or something, so at least they could have kept in touch over the long hours before they saw each other again. But even if she had…they needed to have this conversation in person.

She just hated waiting for it.

Finally, the morning sun slipped through the curtains of her hotel suite, and she allowed herself to get up and dressed. She chose a sundress more like the ones she'd worn in Switzerland, rather than one of the more formal outfits Gianna had packed for her; she didn't want to be Princess Isabella today. Not with Matteo.

Perhaps he had been unable to sleep, too, because when she snuck downstairs for the first breakfast serving, uncomfortably aware of her security team following her as she went, he was already seated at a table in the corner.

The hotel staff tried to usher her towards a private seating area, offering to bring her whatever breakfast foods she desired, but Isabella sent them away with a smile. She wanted to choose her own food, from the buffet, just as all the other guests would be doing; otherwise, she might as well have had breakfast alone in her room. Which, now she thought about it, was probably what the hotel staff—not to mention her security team and her brother—would have preferred.

Before Lake Geneva, that was exactly what she would have done. But things were different now.

Isabella motioned the bodyguard flanking her towards an unoccupied table in the corner, indicating that she'd follow shortly when she'd chosen her food. The buffet was in clear line of sight from the table, so he didn't object.

Helping herself to a plate, Isabella lingered by the watery scrambled eggs, and waited to see if Matteo would take the hint.

'You know, I could take you to about seven different cafés in walking distance of this hotel that would do you a better breakfast than this.' His voice, low and familiar by her ear, sent a warmth coursing through her that had nothing to do with summer.

'Then maybe you should,' she murmured back. 'Any suggestions on how I might get out of here alone, though?' She didn't risk a glance over her shoulder at her bodyguard, probably watching their every move.

Matteo didn't even pause to think; she suspected he'd been planning this all morning. 'The corner by the coffee station is hidden from sight, but there's another door out that way. Go get some coffee, and I'll distract your security guy. When you can see he's occupied, slip out the side door of the hotel and meet me there. I'll be as quick as I can; just stay out of sight.'

She nodded, to show that she'd heard him, then picked up her plate and headed for the coffee station, while Matteo walked away in the other direction. Giving her bodyguard a smile, she lifted a coffee cup from the stack to show her intention.

Her heart was racing at the idea of actually following through with the plan. But, she reminded herself, she wasn't just taking this risk for herself. It was for the baby that might be growing inside her right now.

That was most definitely worth taking risks for.

'Hey, aren't you Matteo Rossi?' she heard her bodyguard say as she ducked into the coffee area.

Smiling to herself, she listened to Matteo agreeing to sign an autograph, and getting into a deep discussion about his teammates' chances in the next Grand Prix, then slipped out of the promised door and headed for freedom.

She tucked herself behind a pillar just outside the hotel and waited. Matteo joined her not long after, grabbing her arm and taking off at a steady clip around the back of the hotel. 'Come on.'

Isabella wasn't even properly surprised when she found herself on the back of a motorcycle, a few moments later, a black helmet crammed over her head and her arms wrapped tight around Matteo's waist as he took off through the streets of Rome.

A wonderful sense of freedom, one she hadn't felt since she'd left Lake Geneva, rushed over her with the wind. This, this was what she'd been missing. Well, this and everything Matteo had given her on the balcony the night before…and everything else she wanted from him. Was it the motorcycle or him making her throb between her thighs?

Probably both, she decided as he swung around another corner and finally pulled to a halt.

'Where are we?' she asked, pulling off her helmet, and hoping her hair wasn't completely wrecked. She ran her fingers through her tangled curls and hoped for the best.

'Just around the corner from the Forum, and the Coliseum.' Matteo shrugged. 'I figured we can walk and talk, you can see a little history, and then we'll get pizza before I take you back. Sound okay?'

Isabella nodded. Leaving the bike parked in a side street, helmets attached, they headed out into the historical centre of Rome. Matteo held out a hand to her and she took it, conscious as they joined the streams of tourists wandering the ancient, excavated streets of the Forum that they could be any other couple, enjoying a summer's day in Rome.

The only thing that ruined the illusion was the tension in Matteo's shoulders, and the way she couldn't help but check over her shoulder for any sign of the palace security team catching up with them.

'So,' Matteo said, after a while of just wandering amongst the ruins. 'I guess we need to talk.'

He'd chosen a good place for it, she realised belatedly. Here in the open air, with so much conversation and chatter, and people moving past them all the time, who was there to listen in on such an intensely private conversation? And who would realise the consequences of it, even if they *did* listen?

In a restaurant, they might have been photographed together, or recognised by a waitress who later sold her story. Matteo was far more famous here than she was—her bodyguard had proved that—but with his cap pulled low over his face, hopefully no one would recognise him.

She took a deep breath. 'Yes, we do.'

'Are you sure?' he asked, and she looked at him with confusion until he shook his head and clarified. 'Not about talking. I mean, about… have you taken a test?'

'Not yet,' she admitted. 'It's not the easiest thing to do with the whole palace watching you.'

'Right. Do you…do you want to? I could find a pharmacy…'

Isabella sighed. 'I'll need to, soon. But for now… I'm over a week late, Matteo. I think we have to assume it's likely, given our last night together in Switzerland.'

That damn broken condom. Although, without it, would she even be here, in Rome, exploring with Matteo like a tourist? She doubted it. More likely, she'd be still locked up in the palace, itching to escape but not knowing where or how.

At least this had focused her. Shown her how much the freedom she'd found with Matteo had given her.

She'd already known how much she'd missed him.

'Yeah. So…assuming you are…'

'Pregnant,' she said, since it seemed that he couldn't.

'What do you want to do next?'

And wasn't that the million-euro question?

'I… If there's a baby, I want to keep it.' That part was easy. However hard it might be, however scandalised Augustan society, however furious her family. This was her baby, and no one could take that away from her. 'Is that a problem?'

Matteo looked horrified. 'I wasn't suggesting—I didn't mean—Isabella, *of course* I support you if you want to keep the baby. I guess all I meant was… I'll be guided by you on this. It's your body, your choice.'

Your reputation, he didn't add, but Isabella could hear it in the air between them, all the same.

She wouldn't have risked it for anything else, they both knew that. But a baby…that changed things.

'What about you?' she asked, to drive the thought away. 'Would you want to be involved? Or even acknowledged? I mean, nobody has to know, if you don't want to be part of this.'

Grabbing her hands, Matteo yanked her out of the path, against a crumbling ruin of a wall, and met her gaze with his own, intense green one.

'Bella. If you are pregnant with my child, of course I will be a part of that. I'll marry you in a heartbeat if you'll let me—or if the King and Queen will, I suppose. Having a family with you will be my next big adventure, I guess.' He flashed her a quick smile at that, but it did nothing to diminish the seriousness of what he was offering.

If she was pregnant, he would marry her. Because for all that he was a reckless, daredevil playboy, he was also a good man. He'd do the right thing.

Even if he didn't want to.

And that was the problem. There'd been no mention of love, in any of his grand declaration. If she hadn't come to Rome and told him about the possibility of the baby, would he have ever come to find her? She wasn't exactly difficult to locate—The Palace, Augusta would probably do it on a map search, or even a letter.

Matteo had given her a freedom she'd never experienced in her whole, pampered princess life. She wasn't going to take his away now, just to save a few shreds of her royal reputation.

So instead of the shock of an Italian racing-car driver stealing away their Princess, the Augustan crown and public might have to deal with having an unmarried single mother in the royal succession—if she was even allowed to keep her title, which was not a sure thing at all. Her stomach was cramping just thinking about her brother's reaction.

She knew she could lose everything, the

same way Aunt Josephine had, and she might not even have true love to show for it.

'Let's find a pharmacy. Buy a test. Then we can plan. After pizza.'

Matteo *really* hoped nobody had recognised him buying a pregnancy test. But who else could he ask to do it? If he was recognised, at least no one would connect it to Isabella yet. If *she* was recognised, well… That was a whole different matter.

There was nothing to link him and the Princess of Augusta. Not until they announced their engagement, anyway.

Don't think about it.

It was the right thing to do, he knew that. For Isabella, and for their child. And for him, too, really. He wanted to be a part of his son or daughter's life, the way his own father never had, and if that child was Augustan royalty then the only way he was getting close was by living up to his responsibilities and marrying their mother.

He just didn't like the way his whole body clenched at the idea of being tied down as somebody's *husband*. Would he still be allowed to race? To live his life the way he wanted? He had a sneaky suspicion that his cliff-diving days would be limited, once he was inaugurated into the Augustan royal family.

If they'd even have him.

Would he cost Isabella her title by marrying her? It wasn't as if he couldn't afford to support her in the manner she was accustomed to—his billions would go a long way to providing compensation, as would, he hoped, the freedom they'd have to live their lives together unencumbered by the royal rules, if she was thrown out of the royal family.

But being a Princess of Augusta was her birthright. Giving up her country was something she wouldn't have even considered if it weren't for him. No, if it weren't for the baby.

They managed to sneak back into Isabella's hotel room by a similar distraction technique to earlier in the day. Matteo would have less respect for the security team for falling for it a second time except this time around Isabella was the distraction. With their apologetic wayward charge back in hand, all attention was on her explanation for her disappearance, leaving Matteo free to sneak into her room with the key card she'd given him.

She joined him a few minutes later, rolling her eyes as she shut the door to keep her latest bodyguard firmly outside the room.

'Okay?' Matteo asked softly as he emerged from his hiding place by the wardrobe.

'Fine. They just all think I'm still sixteen or something. I'm under orders to stay here for the rest of the evening.' She stalked towards him, a predatory grin on her face. 'Which shouldn't be a problem, since you're here with me.'

The pregnancy test burning a hole in his pocket was totally forgotten when she smiled at him like that. But as she pushed his light summer jacket from his shoulders, it fell out onto the floor, a stark reminder to them both of why they were there.

'Do you want to take that now?' Matteo stepped away, giving her the space to decide.

He could see the warring thoughts fluttering across her face. She bent to pick up the box, pulled out the instruction leaflet, and scanned the text.

'It says it's best to do it first thing in the morning. I'll take it then. I mean, at this point, another few hours aren't going to make any difference. And I want—'

She broke off, and Matteo waited.

'I want to enjoy this last night. Before everything changes.'

He could hear the hesitancy in her voice. She wasn't any surer about this situation than he was, and who could blame her?

But the thing that had blossomed between them during their week on Lake Geneva was still as present and sure as it ever had been—hadn't he felt that last night, on the balcony?

Matteo knew what others might think and say. They'd believe that his actions the night before—attempting to seduce an honest-to-God princess in a semi-public setting—were all about the risk, the same as all of his other extra-curricular activities. But they'd be wrong. It hadn't been the risk that had him hard and desperate in the dark.

It was Isabella. Only ever Isabella.

And she was right; once she took that test and they knew for sure, everything would change. One of them would lose their dreams, their future. Either his racing career and adventurous lifestyle, or her title and her country.

But not yet. They had one last night together.

'You'll have to be very quiet,' he said, thinking of the security team waiting outside her hotel suite door. 'Do you think you can manage that?'

'I did last night, didn't I?' she asked, one eyebrow raised.

He took a step closer, and she echoed it, leaving the pregnancy test on the table behind her. 'Last night, I couldn't do half the things I wanted to do to you. Definitely not enough to make you scream.' And he'd dreamt all night of how different that might have been. If he'd been able to lift that heavy ballgown and kneel under the skirt and take his mouth to her…

'Well, maybe I'll need to fill my mouth with something to keep me quiet.' She kept her gaze trained on his as she dropped to her knees. 'Besides, I think it might actually be *you* who needs to try not to make any noise.'

There was no blood left in his brain, or anywhere except south of his belt. He didn't care about the inadequate thin curtains over the window, or the men outside the door who were trained to break him in two in a moment. All Matteo could concentrate on was Isabella's small hands unfastening his jeans, sliding them down his thighs with his boxers, until he kicked off his shoes and stepped out of them.

Then it wasn't just her hands on him. Shaking her long, dark curls away from her face, she nuzzled against the top of his thighs, pressing soft kisses against his hardness.

God. He was going to lose his mind. He was going to actually go insane with want—and if he didn't, if she did something about it, he was going to scream and get himself killed by her bodyguard.

He had to admit, it didn't sound like a bad way to go.

'You okay up there?' she murmured against his hardness, and he felt her words vibrate through him.

'More than,' he answered honestly.

'Good.' Then, with one last kiss against his thigh, she closed her mouth over the tip of him, and Matteo decided right there and then that this was *definitely* worth dying for.

Staggering back a couple of steps, he grabbed hold of the chair behind him for support, sinking into it as Isabella explored and tasted him to her heart's content. And his, for that matter. Finally, as his body started to tighten, he pulled her away before everything was over too soon for his liking.

'You don't want me to finish? Was it not okay?' She looked up at him, her mouth plump and slick and red but her eyes uncertain.

'It was perfect,' he assured her. 'I just don't want it to end so soon.'

She smiled at that, a catlike, satisfied smile. 'What would you like instead, then?'

He pulled her up into his lap, stripping her sundress over her head before letting her divest him of his shirt. 'I'd rather like to be inside you,' he whispered against her collarbone, and felt her shiver at his words.

She was wet and ready for him when he touched her, and it was only when she stood up to strip off her lingerie that his mind could work well enough to remember the essentials. 'Wait. Condoms.'

Isabella gave him a look as if to say, *Do you really think they're necessary at this point?*

He shrugged. 'No point taking unnecessary risks,' he said, which made her laugh. 'There are some in my wallet.'

She bent over to retrieve his wallet from his jeans on the floor, and Matteo was happily enjoying the view when he heard the first noises outside. Voices. Then a bang on the door.

'Isabella!' The voice outside didn't sound patient. Or happy. 'Let me in this instant!'

CHAPTER TWELVE

ISABELLA SPUN AROUND to face Matteo, still slumped in the chair watching her, his eyes wide. 'It's Leo!'

Because of course it was.

'Your brother?' Matteo kept his voice low, and she nodded in response.

'You need to hide!'

He'd hoped his days of hiding from angry older brothers were over when he became an actual adult, but apparently not. Scooping up his clothes, wallet and—in a brief flash of inspiration—the pregnancy test, Matteo let himself be bundled into the bathroom by Isabella.

'One moment!' she called out cheerily. 'I'm just changing.'

'Isabella, I swear to God—' Whatever Leo was swearing was cut off into a mumble, probably around the time the Crown Prince realised that *anyone* could be listening. Including the press—or at least people who'd sell the video or audio to the papers.

Isabella pulled her dress back over her head and surveyed the room.

'Bella,' Matteo whispered as she pushed the bathroom door closed. 'Remember, you're an adult. He might be a prince, but you're a princess. You get to make your own decisions. No crown can take that away from you, okay?'

Biting down on her lip, she nodded, but Matteo could tell she didn't fully believe him.

He sighed, and sat down on the toilet seat to wait, glad that the door hadn't closed all the way. He was still sitting in almost complete darkness, but at least there was that sliver of light from the bedroom. *And* it meant he could hear what Isabella and her brother were saying.

'Where were you today?' Leo asked, the moment Isabella opened the door.

Matteo hadn't spent much time with him at the ball the other night, and his attention had definitely been elsewhere, but he'd seen enough photos to be able to imagine the Crown Prince's face right then. Red, flustered and angry.

'You skipped out on your security, didn't leave word where you were going, wouldn't answer your phone—'

'I'm sorry.' The apology sounded automatic

to Matteo's ears. As if she was so used to saying it, it was nothing more than a reflex.

Plus he happened to know that she really *wasn't* sorry for running out with him. Not if what they'd been doing before Leo banged on the door was any sign.

'My security team…they're not in any trouble, are they? Because I really didn't give them any choice. I just… I wanted to get outside, get some air. See a little of Rome, that was all. You know how rarely I leave the palace these days.' She was trying to mollify him, to earn his sympathy, but Matteo didn't know Leo well enough to guess whether it would work.

He *did* notice, however, that his habit of asking for forgiveness, not permission, seemed to be rubbing off on his Princess.

'And you know why that is,' Leo shot back. Matteo heard him sigh, then the sound of bed springs creaking, as if he'd sat down on the edge of the bed in exhaustion. 'Bella…people were worried. *I* was worried. You don't know this city, or anybody here. Anything could have happened to you. What if some brigand had recognised you and snatched you off the street?'

'Brigand?' Isabella asked, sounding amused.

'You know what I mean,' Leo snapped back. 'The point is, you weren't *safe*. And while you're here in Rome with me, it's my responsibility to keep you safe.'

'I know. I'm sorry. It's just…what if I didn't want to be safe, all the time?'

There, hidden in that question, was the Isabella *Matteo* knew. The one he wanted, more than any other woman he'd ever met before. The one who made him laugh and chase her and think.

The one who wanted to live a life that was more than being afraid all the time, or doing what other people wanted her to, rather than what she wanted herself.

The woman he might marry, soon. Might spend his whole life with.

It was just a glimmer, though. A brief flash of the woman he'd known in Lake Geneva, who he'd seduced on a balcony the night before. One that was soon smothered by her brother's next words.

'Of course you want to be safe, Isabella. Don't be stupid.'

'Yes. Right. Of course, I do. I'm sorry, Leo. I don't know what I was thinking.'

And with that, all of Matteo's hopes about who she could be if she was just willing to take the chance disappeared.

Maybe inside, Isabella wanted to be free, wanted to live her own life at last. But her family would always stomp out the first flames of rebellion, and she would always let them. She'd build up those walls brick by brick, all by herself, to hold onto her place in the royal family.

She didn't want to be pregnant with his child; her horrified reaction the night the condom had split had made that perfectly clear. She didn't want to have to marry him—it was just the least unacceptable option to her family, and their royal expectations.

He'd marry her, if she was pregnant, because he owed her that. But he had no illusions any more that it would be what either of them wanted. Now, they enjoyed each other's company, the sex was amazing and, yes, he knew he could fall for her. Hard.

But if they married…

He'd be tied into a life he didn't want to live. And she'd be embarrassed by him forever, even if marrying him didn't cost her the title of Princess. He wasn't what anyone wanted for her—even Isabella herself.

Outside, the royal siblings were still talking.

'Look, I know we can all seem a little over-protective at times, Bella,' Leo said. 'But you know why that is. You just don't understand the world outside the palace and, honestly, I'm not sure you want to. We just want to keep you safe, okay?'

'I know that,' Isabella replied, softly. 'I'm sorry.'

The bed springs creaked again. Leo was standing up. 'Don't cry, Bella. It's okay. Just… stay where we can keep you safe. Yeah?'

'Yeah.'

There was quiet for a long moment, before Matteo heard the door to the suite open and close again. He waited.

Isabella's eyes were red when she opened the door. 'I'm sorry you had to hear that.'

Maybe it was just as well that he had. At least it told him exactly what the future held for him.

He held out the pregnancy test. 'I think maybe you'd better take this now. Don't you?'

Negative.

How could it be negative?

'Could it be a false result?' Matteo's voice was tense as he sat beside her on the bed, but she was sure she heard relief in it, all the same.

Isabella shook her head. 'I mean, it *could*, but…'

She could feel it now, those telltale signs she'd been ignoring all day. The slight cramp in her lower back. The tiredness. The stupid tears when she'd been talking to Leo.

Her period was on its way.

She wasn't pregnant.

She might not have proof for another day or so, but she knew it, inside.

'I'm pretty sure it's right,' was all she said.

Matteo let out a long, relieved breath. 'Okay. Well, that's good. Right?'

'Absolutely.' She hadn't wanted to be pregnant—not now, not with a man she'd barely known a few weeks, with whom she had nothing in common outside the bedroom. A man her family would disapprove of on principle. A man who could cost her everything.

So why did she feel like crying?

Period hormones. That's all.

No, that *wasn't* all, and she wasn't going to pretend that it was.

'You okay?' Matteo asked. Of course, *he* looked fine. He didn't have stupid hormones. And he wasn't going back to a life trapped behind palace walls, never daring to reach out for what he wanted from the world, in case it turned on him. In case it destroyed his family, or his reputation.

Really, she'd had a narrow escape. She should be celebrating.

'I'm fine.' It came out as almost a sob. 'Happy tears,' she lied.

'Right.' He didn't look convinced. 'So… what now?'

'You're free,' she said, with a shrug. 'No need to worry about me.'

'And you're just going to go back to the palace as if nothing ever happened?' His tone was even, his expression blank. But Isabella could still feel the tension between them.

'What else can I do?' She was a Princess of Augusta. The privileges that gave her came with a cost—and a lot of expectation. 'I've already pushed about as far as I can coming here, especially so soon after my Switzerland trip. And it's a miracle nobody caught onto that, either.'

She shuddered at the thought of Leo bursting into her suite asking, 'What's this about you spending a week having sex with a racing-car driver in Lake Geneva?'

'I thought…' Matteo looked away, as if he wasn't going to finish his sentence. And suddenly it was vitally important to Isabella that she know *exactly* what he thought.

Because he was the first person in her life who had got to know her as a woman, not a princess. Who hadn't cared about titles or palaces or money. Who hadn't held expectations for what she should do and who she should be. Who loved risk enough to be with her anyway, even when it looked as if they might have been caught out by it.

His opinion mattered, more than almost anyone else's. She needed to hear it.

'What did you think?'

He sighed. Then he looked up from where his hands were clasped between his legs as he sat on the edge of the bed and met her gaze head-on.

'I thought that Lake Geneva had meant something. That coming here had meant something. To you, I mean. And not about me, particularly. I thought—I hoped—that it would be your first step out from under your family's thumb. That you might finally forgive yourself for what happened with that reporter and move on with your life.'

'I came here to tell you I might be having your baby.' Isabella swallowed, his words ringing in her ears. 'If that's not flying in the face of all my family's beliefs and expectations, I don't know what is.'

'And now that you're not? What are you going to do now that you're not pregnant, Isabella?'

She didn't know. She hadn't thought this far. Hadn't thought beyond finding him again, telling him about the baby.

Letting him figure out what she should do next, the way she'd always relied on her family to.

But he had no stake in her future now. No investment in what happened to her next.

She could go back to the palace, to her old life, but she already knew how stifling that felt, now she'd experienced something more. Last time, after everything had happened with Nate, she'd been so grateful for the safety of the palace, the security of her family around her, an impenetrable barrier against the real world outside that only seemed to want to hurt her.

This time...this time it was different. She was comparing her experience with Nate and her time with Matteo as if they were the same, but they weren't. Beyond the fact that they both included her having sex with a man the palace wouldn't approve of...the details were worlds apart.

Matteo didn't want to hurt her. Matteo could be trusted, even if his attitude to risk and opinions on suitable behaviour for a princess would scandalise the whole royal family. He was on *her* side; Nate had never been.

And she knew, now, that she'd never been truly in love with Nate. She wasn't a hundred per cent sure she could say the same about Matteo.

So what *was* she going to do now? What *could* she do?

'I need to go back to Augusta with Leo,' she said, thinking aloud. 'And obviously you don't now need to come with me. We don't need to go tell my parents I'm pregnant and they have to let us get married.' She flashed him a smile at that, ignoring the pang in her heart at the idea. He didn't smile back.

'So you just go back to your old life, and I go back to mine?'

'I guess.' Except that felt so wrong, Isabella knew it wouldn't work. Not for her, anyway. But maybe that was what Matteo wanted? His old life back—racing and risks and other women. 'Is that what you want?'

His smile was sad. 'I'm trying to find out what *you* want, Princess.'

When was the last time someone had asked her what she wanted and actually listened to the answer? Even the staff serving dinner at the palace brought her whatever dish the diet plan her mother's nutritionist had set her said she should eat, rather than what she actually fancied.

But Matteo was asking, and she knew he meant it.

What did she want? She wanted everything. He'd taught her the value of taking a risk, when it was the *right* risk. And maybe there was a way she could do it that wouldn't ruin everything else, too.

She took a breath, and a risk, and answered him honestly.

'I want to see you again. I want to *keep* seeing you. I don't want to say goodbye.'

Matteo's heart lurched in his chest as she spoke the words he'd been hoping—though not expecting—to hear. But before he could answer, she went on.

'I mean, we'd need to keep it a secret. God only knows what Leo would say if he found out. But we've managed this far, right? I think as long as I stay out of trouble at the palace, or when I'm with my family, nobody is going to mind if I take the odd weekend off. We can plan ahead, arrange to meet places where no one knows either of us. I might need to speak with Gianna about my security team...'

She had it all figured out, Matteo realised. Exactly how to have her cake and eat it.

Or have him, and not disappoint her family.

And it *should* be perfect. It should be exactly what he wanted. The freedom to live his life how he wanted and still see Isabella, without getting tied into her world and the expectations that went with it.

So why did his chest ache so much?

Because I'm not enough for her.

Ever since he was a teenager, he'd tried to live enough for two, to make up for everything

Giovanni had lost. He'd done more, seen more, risked more than most people on the planet.

But he still wasn't enough for Isabella.

'Matteo?' She looked up at him, a tiny line forming between her eyebrows.

'I can't.' Pushing up off the bed, he paced across to the window. 'Isabella... I can't just be some dirty secret for you, the guy you're ashamed to bring home to your family.'

Her eyes widened at that, and she reached out towards him before sitting on her hands. 'That wasn't... I didn't mean it that way.'

'I know.' He sighed. 'But...when you told me you thought you were pregnant, I was scared, sure. But excited too. Because honestly? I've never felt anything like what I feel for you for any woman before now. I thought that maybe we could make this work. Until I heard you talking to your brother.'

'Leo? You can't... I just had to say whatever he needed to hear to get him out of here, before he found you hiding in my bathroom!'

'Yeah, but you meant it, too. And if I'd doubted it at all...you just confirmed it now.' God, he hated saying this. Hated thinking this. Realising it was true.

After so many years of pushing love away, of keeping it at arm's length to avoid the inevitable losses that came with it...now he found himself here. Wanting, wishing for a princess's love—and knowing that he couldn't take the loss that came with it when she didn't love him enough in return.

He'd been looking for an excuse to upend his whole life for her—to make her upend her life for him. But if she really wasn't pregnant, that excuse was gone. And he wasn't such a terrible human as to try again and bring a baby into a relationship they didn't have the courage to seek anyway.

He had honestly believed there was no risk he wouldn't take. Turned out that loving Princess Isabella of Augusta when she didn't love him was the line he couldn't cross.

'I'm not saying we *never* tell them,' she tried, but Matteo shook his head.

'It's okay, Isabella. We never—this wasn't ever the love match M wanted it to be. We weren't matched together because we were soulmates who were going to live happily ever after. We were put together because my manager wanted to keep me out of trouble and your assistant wanted to give you a week off from being a princess.'

'It was more than that,' she said softly.

'Was it?' Because it was hard to remember that right now.

'You know it was.'

'It was great sex, I'll give you that.' His heart was breaking, but he knew he couldn't give in. Couldn't let her say anything that would persuade him to stay. To hide away and follow her rules instead of his own.

For seventeen years he'd worked every day to fulfil his late brother's ambitions. To cross off every item on the bucket list he'd written before he died. And now, here he was, thirty-three years old and no idea what he wanted from his future for himself. Nothing except a half-scribbled list of adventures still to be had.

But he knew what he didn't want. And surely that was a pretty good place to start.

'Isabella, think about it. We sneak around, we have some fun, and, sure, I'm not denying I want that too—I want more time with you. But it wouldn't be enough. Not for me.' He'd never been the marrying type. Until he met Isabella. 'Eventually, the secrecy would break us. Or we'd get found out, and you'd have to choose. Your family, your title, or me. We dodged a bullet, this time. I won't put us in front of another one.'

'So what? We just never see each other again?' There were tears in her eyes. Matteo had to look away.

'I think it's for the best.' Even if it broke his heart. 'I can't live by your royal rules, even if they'd have me. I can't hide away my love for you, either. I need to go out there and live my life—not yours, not my brother's—just mine. I'm sorry.'

He didn't kiss her goodbye. Couldn't even meet her gaze.

Instead, he walked straight out of the hotel suite, and pretended not to see the astonished look from the bodyguard as he headed back to his old life once more.

CHAPTER THIRTEEN

ISABELLA SLIPPED HER sunglasses over her eyes as she stepped out of the car at the small airfield outside the city. She'd pretended to sleep during the short drive out there—believable, given the early start—but now she needed something else to hide her red-rimmed eyes from her brother.

Not that he was looking at her, of course. He had work to do: emails from the prime minister, or something. Leo was being groomed to take over the throne, possibly sooner rather than later if their father decided he'd like to step aside and retire to the country. It wasn't unprecedented in Augustan history, and King Leonardo *had* been looking tired recently.

Musing on royal successions distracted her brain from the only other topic it seemed able to hold until they were seated on the royal plane at last. But then, as they prepared for take-off, it occurred to her that once Leo became King her role would be even less clear.

Her brother had married three years ago in a royal pageant like none the country had seen before. His wife, Princess Serena, was still in Augusta with their adorable toddler son, pregnant with their next child already. The succession was secure, and Isabella was happy for it. The further she got from the throne, the less pressure on her to be perfect.

But since she *was* further from the throne… what was the point of her? As a princess, at least? Serena had happily taken over a lot of the public-facing duties; the daughter of an ex-prime minister and a famously beautiful duchess, she was used to the spotlight. She was also a huge favourite with the Augustan people, mostly for having cute babies, but also for her keen fashion sense and ability to look empathetic on demand.

Isabella just wore whatever Gianna told her to wear. And, having grown up in a palace, was generally seen as unable to empathise with the Augustan public, even more than a woman who'd also had nannies from birth and gone to the same boarding school.

The point was, there was no place for her in Leo's new palace. If her father *did* hand over the crown sooner rather than later, would she even be welcome to stay there? Or would she move to the country with her parents, a spin-ster princess for ever?

More likely, they'd marry her off to some duke or lord they needed support from for something. Because Augusta liked nothing more than tradition—and the tradition of using princesses as pawns was well established.

Are you just going to do what they tell you for ever? The words sounded in her head in Matteo's voice.

Suddenly, she had to know.

'Leo.'

Her brother looked up from his papers and his laptop, his reading glasses perched on the end of his nose, and irritation in his eyebrows. 'Yes?'

'When you become King, what happens to me?'

'What do you mean? You can carry on as you always have.' He looked back down at his papers.

'No, I mean… What role do I play in the country?' she pressed.

Sighing, Leo removed his glasses and rubbed his temples. 'You want to talk about this now?'

Isabella shrugged. 'We're not going any-where. Why not now?'

'Because you haven't shown any interest in your future, or how you can support the country or the monarchy, in years. So I'll ask again, why now?'

'That's not true.' The words were automatic, but they didn't quite cover the sinking feeling in Isabella's stomach that, actually, it might be. 'I care about our country. I do the public appearances I have to. I smile for the cameras. I stay out of trouble... Just because I haven't married any of the titled idiots you keep throwing my way—'

Leo cut her off with a weary sigh. 'Bella... Do you really not get it? After everything that happened with that reporter chap—'

'None of you trust me to make my own decisions! Trust me, I get it. I have to follow The Rules, more than anyone else, because I can't be relied on to choose good people, to know who to trust. To fall in love responsibly.' As if she could ever have missed that.

Even after all the stories about Aunt Josephine, she might have had hope that Augusta was changing with the times.

If it hadn't been for everything that had happened with Nate, maybe she'd have had the courage to take Matteo home to meet her parents. To tell them that, while he might not be the Augustan lord they'd hoped she'd marry, she loved him, and she hoped she had their blessing—but she'd marry him without, if he'd have her.

If there'd been a baby, they'd have had to let her. But now…she knew they'd remind her of her past mistakes and steer her away from what she thought could make her happy.

'That's not… Bella, it's not that we don't trust you.' Leo sounded amazed that she could even think it, which, considering the number of lectures he'd given her over the years on the 'right sort', was a bit rich.

'Of course, it is—' she started, but Leo kept talking over her.

'It's that you don't trust *yourself.*'

She fell silent.

Oh. *Oh.* Leo's words resonated in her ribcage until she couldn't deny the truth of them.

All these years, she'd thought she was toeing the royal line for them. Because it was what she needed to do to have their love, their faith. To keep her position.

And Leo had torn that away with just one line.

She'd been using The Rules as an excuse, thinking she was protecting her reputation, her family—but in truth, she'd been protecting her heart.

'Do you blame me?' she asked, slumping down in her seat to consider the implications of this revelation. 'The last time I thought I was in love, I almost brought down the monarchy.'

Leo chuckled. 'I don't think it was quite *that* bad. Although at the time, I was a little worried that the prime minister was going to have a heart attack.'

'So why all the awful set-up dates with your friends and other lords?' Because she definitely hadn't imagined those.

'Because… Bella, after everything that happened, you sort of drew in on yourself. You shut yourself up in the palace, avoided as many public events as you could, and only spent time with people you'd known practically since birth—like Sofia, or Gianna. We were worried about you. So yes, we tried to get you back out there—to help you get some confidence back—by getting you to spend time with people we knew we could trust. And yes, I can't deny that we were hoping you'd find love with one of them. Because we want you to be *happy*, and you so obviously weren't.'

Isabella looked quickly out of the window, so her brother wouldn't see the tears in her eyes. 'I thought it was because you didn't trust me.'

'It was because we loved you. And we wanted you to trust yourself again. To find your way back to us.' Leo sighed. 'But apparently we only pushed you further away. Serena warned me…well, never mind that now. The important thing is, when I am King, the same as now, there will always be a place for you in my palace, if you want it.'

'Thank you, Leo,' she said softly. 'And…and I think that, maybe, I'm ready to do a little more for the family business, so to speak. If you want me?'

'If?' Leo laughed. 'Serena would *love* it if you could take some of her events and visits off her plate right now. This pregnancy is exhausting her even more than the last, and I've been worried about her trying to do so much.'

Guilt twinged in her chest. 'I'm sorry. I should have noticed—should have offered sooner.'

Reaching across the aisle between them, Leo took her hand. 'None of that. We're all at fault for not realising things sooner. Not talking about them. I know our parents…they're a different generation, and for them feelings are very private, not to be discussed. But it doesn't have to be like that for us, Bella. I'm always here if you want to talk.'

She smiled, although it felt weak on her lips.

Maybe she'd never be what Matteo wanted—she couldn't stop being a princess, and she didn't *want* to walk away from her heritage, her country. Quite the opposite. She was finally ready to take her proper place and do her part—and it seemed that Leo would let her.

'You said "last time", before,' Leo said cautiously. 'The last time you fell in love. Does that mean…? Is there someone you think you might—?'

'No.' She cut him off quickly. 'That's not… don't worry about that.'

The lines on Leo's forehead told her that he *was* worrying. Isabella sighed.

'I met someone when I was in Switzerland I thought might…but he didn't want the royal life. Or me.' All the truth, even if Leo still believed her trip to Geneva was to visit their cousin Sofia. It was plausible that she might have met someone there, and she wasn't quite ready to confess *everything* to her brother, yet.

'Are you sure? Because, Bella, you put up walls. One day you're going to have to let someone in. And when you do, I'll support you. Whoever they are.'

But she had, hadn't she? That was the problem. She'd let Matteo all the way in. She'd been so afraid of falling in love again, and now it had happened she could see why.

Except that following The Rules meant she'd be heartbroken for ever, separated from the man she finally admitted to herself that she loved. Completely and totally.

She couldn't regret her time with him, even now he'd walked away from her because of who she was. Because loving Matteo had shown her that love was worth taking risks for.

'What about Aunt Josephine?' she asked suddenly, remembering all the stories that had swirled around the palace. 'You said "whoever they are" but that wasn't true for her, was it?'

Leo's brows met in a puzzled frown. 'Aunt Josephine… Bella, she left the palace before you were even born!'

'Was driven out, you mean. Because the King and Queen—our grandparents—didn't approve of who she fell in love with.' Everyone knew that.

'Bella, she *chose* to leave. She didn't want the life of pageantry at the palace. She wanted to run a racing stables with her husband, so they left.' He shook his head. 'I know there was a lot of gossip—I heard plenty of it myself. So I sought her out and asked her, and she told me the truth. I guess it didn't occur to you to do the same?' he asked, looking amused.

'Well…no.'

Leo sighed. 'But you're not entirely wrong. Josie knew that there'd be a lot of talk when she married her groom. I'm sure that weighed into her decision to step away from royal life. But I promise you that no one *made* her. And if you fell in love with someone…perhaps not entirely in keeping with royal expectation, we'd find a way to make it work. *I* would make it work for you, if he made you happy. Okay?'

'Okay,' she said, blinking away tears. 'Thank you, Leo.'

'So, with that in mind, are you *sure* there isn't a certain gentleman you'd like me to meet? I can have the pilot divert to Switzerland, if you want? Or return to Rome, perhaps…?' He left the suggestion hanging, and Isabella wondered how much he'd already guessed about the man she loved.

It was so tempting, to head back and find Matteo and tell him they could be together. But Leo was right about Aunt Josephine's decision, too. She'd chosen to move away from the royal life because there *would* be a scandal, and she didn't want to live it.

Whereas Isabella had only just reconfirmed to herself how much she wanted to step back *into* royal life. She loved Matteo, but she had to live her own life, too—just as he needed to live his. And she couldn't decide for him on this one. If he wanted to be part of her royal life, that would be up to him—and without the baby to bind them together, it didn't seem as if he would.

'I can't live by your royal rules, even if they'd

have me.' His words echoed in her brain, and she knew there was no point turning around.

'I'm sure,' she replied to her brother.

Leo gave her a sad smile. 'I'm sorry, Bella. But one day, you'll find the right one.'

Isabella tried to smile, to look as if she believed him. But her heart was telling her that she already had.

She just hadn't been able to hold onto him.

Matteo slammed back into the team hotel, ignoring all the fans and press he passed on the way. No way he was talking to any of them—not after a race like that.

There was, unfortunately, one person he *couldn't* avoid, though.

Gabe slipped into his hotel room behind him, before Matteo could take out his rage on another door.

'So. That was quite a race.'

'It was a disaster.'

'It was definitely close,' Gabe admitted.

Throwing himself into the chair by the window, Matteo put an arm over his eyes, only to find those final moments of the race running behind his eyelids like a video. The way the barrier had seemed to rise up before him. The roar of the other car's engine, too close at his side. The split second when he'd honestly believed that this could be it. The last risk he ever took.

He removed his arm and opened his eyes, to find Gabe perched on the edge of the bed across from him.

'What happened, Matteo?'

'It was a bad race, that's all.' Matteo shook his head. 'That idiot Rennard was too close.'

'There was no penalty given,' Gabe observed, mildly. 'There seemed to be room as he overtook.'

Except he shouldn't have been overtaking in the first place, should he? Matteo had never lost to *Rennard* of all people before now.

He'd lost his nerve, that had to be it. He'd seen that corner and, for the first time, thought about the risks.

Was this what love did to a person? If so, he needed to get over it, fast.

'Matteo...you've not been the same since you came back from Switzerland. I think everyone can see that. It's not just the race,' Gabe added quickly, when Matteo started to object. 'It's *you*. Before, you were happy, racing along through life, living it to the full. Ticking things off Giovanni's list.'

'How did you know about that?' Because Matteo was damn sure he'd never told him. He'd never told anyone except Isabella.

But Gabe just gave him a look. One of those, *When will you learn that I see everything and I know everything?* looks.

'The point is, you're not happy now,' Gabe said. 'Are you?'

'No.' It was hell to admit, but he wasn't.

How could he be unhappy? When he lived and Giovanni didn't? When he'd achieved everything his brother had ever set out to do?

He'd even started ticking things off his own bucket list—booking a trip to swim with sharks, during his next break. He had things to look forward to, a life to live. And, today's race notwithstanding, a career he loved and was great at.

'It's the Princess, isn't it? Isabella.' Because of course Gabe knew that too. He'd even kept her brother occupied while Matteo had whisked her out onto the balcony at the ball. 'You're in love with her.'

'I can't be.' Because she didn't love him back—not enough to go against her family, or her title.

She wouldn't take the risk to be with him. And he…he couldn't take the risk of trying to live someone else's life again. He'd done it for his brother, but once was enough.

'I don't think love works like that, son.' Gabe creaked to his feet—for all that he was only fifteen years older than Matteo—and pressed a hand against his shoulder. 'Trust me on this. If it's love that's the problem, there's only one way to fix it.'

'And that is?'

'Tell her. Talk to her.'

'Don't see how that fixes anything,' Matteo grumbled. All the reasons they weren't together would still be there, after all.

But Gabe gave him a knowing smile. 'You'd be surprised. I saw the way she looked at you in Rome, Matteo. So I don't think the problem here is unrequited love. Which means there's something else keeping you apart. And maybe that something else is insurmountable, I don't know. But what I *do* know is this: once you tell her? Then it's not just you against this thing. It's the two of you, together. And two people in love against the world? I'd back those odds every time.'

With one last squeeze to his shoulder, Gabe let himself out of the room, leaving Matteo thinking in his chair. After a moment, he pulled an already tattered piece of paper out of his pocket and stared at it.

His new bucket list. The one he'd started after Lake Geneva, to replace the one that Giovanni had left him with. He'd been adding to it piecemeal ever since, whenever a new adventure occurred to him.

Now, he read through it and realised something he'd never have believed if someone else had told him.

He didn't care about any of them.

If things had gone the wrong way on the track that day, in that split second when he'd believed it might, he wouldn't regret not having done any of the things on his bucket list. Hell, in that moment he wouldn't have even been able to remember what any of them were.

Because his mind had been filled with only one thought.

The thought that he'd never see Isabella again.

That would be his only regret.

Lurching to his feet, Matteo crushed the paper in his fist. He didn't need it any more. Didn't need a bucket list at all.

She was his list.

He'd been holding onto his freedom, his adventures, but ultimately, what did they matter if he didn't have her?

Maybe he'd never be enough for her, maybe she'd never love him enough to take the chances that were needed for them to be together. But he knew he had to try.

Until today, he'd always risked his body,

freely, happily, loving that surge of adrenaline it gave him. The power over the universe he felt when he survived the odds. Every experience was proof that he'd outwitted the world. That he was *alive*, even if Giovanni wasn't.

But he'd only ever risked his body.

And now, he knew, it was time to risk his heart.

'Are you sure you're okay doing this?' Princess Serena lowered her very pregnant body into her chair and Isabella smiled at the obvious relief her sister-in-law immediately felt.

'Of course. I'm happy to. And at least it's only kids, right?' Some of the children Isabella would be talking to on their visit to the palace rose garden today had been barely walking when she'd embarrassed herself so horribly with Nate. Of course, their teachers would probably remember. But Leo had assured her that most of Augusta had moved on with their lives since then, and forgotten.

It was only Isabella who hadn't. Until now.

'Your Highness? When you're ready?' Gianna called her from the door, and Isabella nodded to tell her she was coming.

Her assistant seemed pleased that she was doing more, too. Isabella supposed it couldn't be much fun organising royal appointments for a princess who refused to do any beyond the odd video interview.

Of course, it was one of those video interviews that had led her here—via Lake Geneva, and Matteo.

As always, her heart twinged at the memory of him. Her period had come and gone as predicted, just two weeks later than planned. Apparently that could be due to stress, which Isabella supposed was possible. Whatever it was, with it the last piece of Matteo that she could have hoped to hold onto was gone too.

Time to start over.

A new life, new responsibilities.

She followed Gianna out along the endless hallways to the rose garden door, taking care to keep her breathing even and her smile in place. Her hair was styled, her simple dress and cardigan polished but not overwhelming for a group of seven-and eight-year-olds. Apparently these were the children from the capital's schools who'd achieved the most over the school year and so, as a treat, they got to spend a day of their summer holidays in school uniform touring the palace—and meeting a real-life princess.

And this year, for the first time in years, that princess was Isabella.

'Ready?' Gianna asked, before she opened the door.

Isabella nodded, and stepped out into the August sunshine, smiling at the crowds of small children and teachers who clapped her appearance, even if she hadn't really done anything yet.

The speech she'd been asked to give had been written for Serena, but Isabella thought she gave it well enough all the same. Talking about doing your best, helping others and working hard—all the things the children were being commended for—reminded her a little too much of how many years she'd spent *not* doing those things. But she was changing that now, and that was something.

Once the speech was over, and cake and drinks were brought out for the children, Isabella spent her time chatting with them, and their teachers, individually—learning more about their lives, about how they viewed their country. It was only a start, but she felt closer to the people her family ruled over than she had in years.

She was so engrossed in her conversations that she only vaguely noticed when Gianna slipped away, after talking with one of the palace guards. And only realised she'd returned when she heard her clear her throat behind her and say, 'Your Highness? I'm sorry to interrupt, but there's someone here to see you.'

The teachers were already chivvying the children back towards their bus; the visit had gone on longer than planned, Isabella knew. She said her goodbyes to the group she was talking to, and turned to see who else wanted to speak with her—

And promptly lost the ability to speak.

'Wait! Aren't you Matteo Rossi? The racing-car driver?' One of the boys who'd been on the school visit had escaped his teacher's grasp and raced back across the grass, promptly followed by most of his friends.

Matteo smiled graciously and signed autographs on request. At least it gave her the chance to gather her thoughts and stop her heart from racing quite so fast at the sight of him.

Why was he here? Hadn't they said everything they needed to when they'd parted? Unless things had changed...but how could they?

She'd changed, though, hadn't she? One conversation with Leo on the plane home from Rome and she'd found a whole new path—and a better understanding of herself, her past, and maybe even her future.

Perhaps the same had happened to him.

Was it wrong of her to hope so?

Eventually, the teachers won the battle to get the children to go home, and the rose garden emptied of people. Even Gianna had found somewhere else to be, and the palace guard were back at their posts, studiously ignoring them.

And so it was just Isabella and Matteo again, as it had been at the start.

'You came,' she said. '*Here*. Why?'

'Because I couldn't go the rest of my life without seeing you again,' Matteo replied. 'In fact, I'm not sure I could go without seeing you every single day for the rest of my life, if it comes to that.'

'I'm not pregnant,' Isabella blurted. 'I mean, I know I said…but definitely. You don't have to marry me to save my honour or anything.'

'I know that.' Matteo's smile was half amused, half fond. 'What else?'

'I'm not going to stop being a princess. I mean, I only just remembered why it's important in the first place.' She couldn't let her hopes get too high, if that was still a deal-breaker.

But Matteo just asked, 'Which is?'

'Because I can do things that matter to me. Help people, raise awareness, support my country. That sort of thing.'

This time, his smile almost split his face. 'Doing things that matter to you is the *only* good reason, I've come to realise, to do anything. To risk everything.'

He stepped closer and she moved into his

arms automatically, as if that was where she belonged. It felt as if she did, anyway.

'So…what now?' she asked.

'I can't be a secret,' Matteo said, his eyes serious. 'If we're together, I need to be able to tell the world. Because hiding it implies there's something wrong or bad about it, and there isn't. I love you, Isabella, and I don't ever want to hide that.'

'I don't, either,' Isabella admitted as the warmth of his words filled her. *He loves me.* 'I hadn't realised how much I'd hidden myself away, how afraid I was to trust my own instincts, to trust *anyone*. I was using my past as an excuse to put up walls. But I trust you, and I know how I feel about you.'

'What will your family think about that?' Matteo asked.

'My parents might be…not thrilled. Especially if you're planning to carry on racing?'

'I am.'

She nodded. Of course, he wouldn't give that up; it was who he was, not just for his late brother, but for himself. And she'd never want to stop him being himself—not when she was only just learning who she wanted to be herself.

'But I've come to see that actually my family do want me to be happy, more than anything else.' And some of the barriers to their relationship might have been in her own head rather than other people's. 'I can't promise it's going to be easy—I mean, a lot of the people in power here are old-school conservative. They'd be happiest if I married a second cousin or something, but…'

'But?'

It had taken a lot of courage to talk to Leo about her future. More to start putting herself back out there again. But this was the real test—and the only one she truly cared about passing.

Isabella took a deep breath. 'But I don't want to marry anyone but you. Because I love you, Matteo Rossi. And I'm willing to take any risk to keep you with me—if you're willing to submit to everything that comes with loving a princess.'

He swept her up into his arms until her toes barely touched the floor, kissing her passionately enough that she didn't need words any more to know how he felt. From behind the rose garden gate, she thought she might have heard a palace guard give a congratulatory whoop.

When she was finally back on solid ground again, she smiled up at him. 'So is that a yes, then?'

Matteo raised an eyebrow. 'Was there a question?'

'Matteo Rossi, will you marry me, and be my Prince?' She batted her eyelashes at him, and he laughed.

'Only if we can honeymoon in Lake Geneva.'

'Deal.'

'And have sex on the balcony again.'

'Definitely.'

'Then, yes, Princess Isabella of Augusta.' He pressed a light, chaste kiss to her lips. 'I'll marry you. Because life without you is one risk I'm just not willing to take.'

EPILOGUE

'I WASN'T SURE, you know,' Leo said as they stood at the front of the Cathedral of Augusta, listening to organ music and the buzz of excitement from the crowd behind them.

'About the outfits?' Matteo guessed, looking down at the traditional Augustan dress he'd been forced into for the occasion. Gabe had laughed out loud at the sight of it until he'd realised that, as Matteo's best man, he'd be required to wear it too.

'About *you*,' Leo clarified. 'I mean, after you stole my sister away at a public ball, then helped her escape her security team to roam about Rome with you...'

Matteo winced. 'She told you that?'

'No. I am just not an idiot.' Leo gave him a long, assessing look, and Matteo was very aware of Gabe not trying very hard to hide his smile beside him. 'I admit, I was not sure about you. But,' he went on, over Matteo's attempts to interrupt, 'I promised my sister that when she found the man she loved, I would support her. Whoever he was.'

'Well, thank you for that, anyway,' Matteo replied. He knew that her brother's support would have gone a way to giving Isabella the confidence she needed to take a chance on him.

'And having you here this week preparing for the wedding, I admit, has helped me change my mind.'

'It has?' Matteo asked, surprised. Especially since he and Isabella had, as much as possible, eschewed wedding prep in favour of getting to know one another all over again, away from that private villa on Lake Geneva. Which had mostly meant hiding away in her private rooms. In bed.

'You love my sister.' Leo shrugged. 'That's all I ever really wanted for her.'

'I do love her,' Matteo admitted. 'More than anything.' That part might have taken him a little while to realise, but now he had, he couldn't believe he'd ever thought otherwise.

They might be from different worlds, and have lived very different lives before they met, but they were a pair. He brought her out from behind her terrified walls, and she helped him find a way to live in the world that didn't mean risking his neck all the time, just to feel alive. To justify his existence.

Oh, he'd still have adventures, and she'd still have days where she needed to hide away. But mostly, they'd have adventures or hide together. Because together, they were so much stronger than they were apart.

And now he got to have that for the rest of his life.

'Good,' Leo said as the organ music changed. 'Because it's time to show the world that.'

Matteo turned as the huge doors to the cathedral creaked open. The pews were filled with the great and good of Augusta, as well as a couple of rows of schoolchildren, and another few of people in uniforms—nurses, soldiers, doctors, police, firefighters. Isabella had insisted on opening the wedding up to the people who really made a difference in her country—and Matteo had supported her.

His friends and teammates were in attendance too, and Matteo sent a quick smile their way before turning his attention to the far end of the aisle. Past the camera crews, broadcasting the occasion live to the world. Past Madison Morgan, smiling with satisfaction in the final pew. To the vision in white appearing on the King's arm as the doors parted.

Isabella glided down the long aisle to sighs

and gasps from the congregation. Matteo stared at her dark curls, pinned up to reveal her long, elegant neck, and the lace neckline of her gown. Below the lace, white silk clung to her curves, down past her hips, before flaring out into a train that was still entering the cathedral when she'd almost reached him at the altar.

Her dark red lips jumped into a nervous smile as she kissed her father on the cheek, then took the last couple of steps alone.

Steps towards *him*. Matteo Rossi—daredevil, racing driver, orphan, world champion. She had chosen *him*. And no race or accolade or adventure had ever made him feel so alive as knowing that Isabella would be at his side for the rest of their lives.

'You look so beautiful,' he whispered as she stood beside him. 'That dress is…'

She flashed him a wicked smile that really had no place in a cathedral. 'Just wait until you see what I'm not wearing under it.'

Beside him Leo made a choking noise, and Gabe stifled a laugh.

Matteo gave thanks for the ridiculous, but concealing, Augustan state dress, and smiled back at his soon-to-be wife. Yeah, being married to a princess was going to be a lot of fun.

* * * * *